LEONETTI'S
HOUSEKEEPER
BRIDE

LEONETTI'S HOUSEKEEPER BRIDE

BY

LYNNE GRAHAM

MILLS & BOON

First published in Great Britain 2016
By Mills & Boon, an imprint of HarperCollins*Publishers*
1 London Bridge Street, London, SE1 9GF

Large Print edition 2016

© 2016 Lynne Graham

ISBN: 978-0-263-26195-0

Our policy is to use papers that are natural, renewable
and recyclable products and made from wood grown
in sustainable forests. The logging and manufacturing
processes conform to the legal environmental regulations
of the country of origin.

Printed and bound in Great Britain
by CPI Antony Rowe, Chippenham, Wiltshire

CHAPTER ONE

GAETANO LEONETTI WAS having a very bad day. It had started at dawn, when his phone went off and proceeded to show him a series of photos that enraged him but which he knew would enrage his grandfather and the very conservative board of the Leonetti investment bank even more. Regrettably, sacking the woman responsible for the story in the downmarket tabloid was likely to be the sole satisfaction he could hope to receive.

'It's not your fault,' Tom Sandyford, Gaetano's middle-aged legal adviser and close friend, told him quietly.

'Of course it's *my* fault,' Gaetano growled. 'It was *my* house, *my* party and the woman in *my* bed at the time who organised the damned party—'

'Celia was that soap star with the cocaine habit

you didn't know about,' Tom reminisced. 'Wasn't she sacked from the show soon after you ditched her?'

Gaetano nodded, his even white teeth gritting harder.

'It's a case of bad luck...that's all,' Tom opined. 'You can't ask your guests to post their credentials beforehand, so you had no way of knowing some of them weren't tickety-boo.'

'Tickety-boo?' Gaetano repeated, his lean, darkly handsome features frowning. Although he was born and raised in England, Italian had been the language of his home and he still occasionally came across English words and phrases that were unfamiliar.

'Decent upstanding citizens,' Tom rephrased. 'So, a handful of them were hookers? Well, in the rarefied and very privileged world you move in, how were you supposed to find that out?'

'The press found it out,' Gaetano countered flatly.

'With the usual silly "Orgy at the Manor" big

reveal. It'll be forgotten in five minutes…although that blonde dancing naked in the fountain out front is rather memorable,' Tom remarked, scanning the newspaper afresh with lascivious intent.

'I don't remember seeing her. I left the party early to fly to New York. Everyone still had their clothes on at that stage,' Gaetano said drily. 'I really don't need another scandal like this.'

'Scandal does rather seem to follow you around. I suppose the old man and the board at the bank are up in arms as usual,' Tom commented with sympathy.

Gaetano compressed his wide sensual mouth in silent agreement. In the name of family loyalty and respect, he was paying in the blood of his fierce pride and ambition for the latest scandal. Letting his seventy-four-year-old grandfather Rodolfo carpet him like a badly behaved schoolboy had proved to be a truly toxic experience for a billionaire whose investment advice was sought by governments both in the UK and abroad. And when Rodolfo had settled into his favourite preaching session about Gaetano's womanising lifestyle, Gaetano had had to breathe in deeply several times and resist the urge to point out to the older man that expectations and values had changed since the nineteen forties for both men *and* women.

Rodolfo Leonetti had married a humble fisherman's daughter at the age of twenty-one and during his fifty years of devoted marriage he had never looked at another woman. Ironically, his only child, Gaetano's father, Rocco, had not taken his father's advice on the benefits of making an early marriage either. Rocco had been a notorious playboy and an incorrigible gambler. He had married a woman young enough to be his daughter when he was in his fifties, had fathered one son and had expired ten years later after over-exerting himself in another woman's bed. Gaetano reckoned he had been paying for his father's sins almost from the hour of his birth. At the age of twenty-nine and one of the world's leading bankers, he was tired of being continually forced to prove his worth and confine his projects to the narrow expectations of the board. He had made millions for the Leonetti Bank; he *deserved* to be CEO.

Indeed, Rodolfo's angry ultimatum that very morning had outraged Gaetano.

'You will *never* be the chief executive of this bank until you change your way of life and settle down into being a respectable family man!' his grandfather had sworn angrily. 'I will not support your leadership with the board and, no matter how brilliant you are, Gaetano, the board *always* listens to me... They remember too well how your father almost brought the bank down with his risky ventures!'

Yet what, realistically, did Gaetano's sex life have to do with his acumen and expertise as a banker? Since when were a wife and children the only measure of a man's judgement and maturity?

Gaetano had not the slightest interest in getting married. In fact he shuddered at the idea of being anchored to one woman for the rest of his life while living in fear of a divorce that could deprive him of half of his financial portfolio. He was a very hard worker. He had earned his academic qualifications with honours in the most prestigious international institutions and his achievements since then had been immense. Why wasn't that enough? In comparison his father had been an academically slow and spoiled rich boy who, like Peter Pan, had refused to grow up. Such a comparison was grossly unfair.

Tom dealt Gaetano a rueful appraisal. 'You didn't get the old "find an ordinary girl" spiel again, did you?'

"'An ordinary girl, *not* a party girl, one who takes pleasure in the *simple* things of life,'" Gaetano quoted verbatim because his grandfather's discourses always ran to the same conclusion: marry, settle down, father children with a home-loving female…and the world would then miraculously become Gaetano's oyster with little happy unicorns dancing on some misty horizon shaped by a rainbow. His lean bronzed features hardened with grim cynicism. He had seen just how well that fantasy had turned out for once-married and now happily divorced friends.

'Perhaps you could time travel back to the nineteen fifties to find this ordinary girl,' Tom quipped, wondering how the era of female liberation and career women had contrived to pass Rodolfo Leonetti by so completely that he still believed such women existed.

'The best of it is, if I did produce an *ordinary* girl and announce that I was going to marry her Rodolfo would be appalled,' Gaetano breathed impatiently. 'He's too much of a snob. Unfortunately he's become so obsessed by his conviction that I need to marry that he's blocking my progression at the bank.'

His PA entered and extended two envelopes. 'The termination of contract on the grounds of the confidentiality clause which has been breached and the notice to quit the accommodation that goes with the job,' she specified. 'The helicopter is waiting for you on the roof, sir.'

'What's going on?' Tom asked.

'I'm flying down to Woodfield Hall to sack the housekeeper who handed over those photos to the press.'

'It was the *housekeeper*?' Tom prompted in surprise.

'She was named in the article. Not the brightest of women,' Gaetano pointed out drily.

Poppy leapt off her bike, kicked the support into place and ran into the village shop to buy milk. As usual she was running late but she could not drink coffee without milk and didn't feel properly awake until she had had at least two cups. Her mane of fiery red-gold curls bounced on her slim black-clad shoulders and her green eyes sparkled.

'Good morning, Frances,' she said cheerfully to the rather sour-looking older woman behind the counter as she dug into her purse to pay.

'I'm surprised you're so bright this morning,'

the shop owner remarked in a tone laden with suggestive meaning.

'Why wouldn't I be?'

The older woman slapped a well-thumbed newspaper down on the counter and helpfully turned it round to enable Poppy to read the head-line. Poppy paled with dismay and snatched the publication up, moving on impatiently to the next page only to groan at the familiar photo of the naked blonde cavorting in the fountain. Her brother, Damien, had definitely taken that photo on the night of that infamous party. She knew that because she had caught him showing that particular one off to his mates.

'Seems your ma has been talking out of turn,' Frances remarked. 'Shouldn't think Mr Leonetti will appreciate that...'

Glancing up to meet the older woman's avidly curious gaze, Poppy hastily paid for the paper and left the shop. That photo? How on earth had the newspaper got hold of it? And what about the other photos? The heaving, fortunately unidentifiable bodies in one of the bedrooms? When invited to join the party by a drunken guest, had Damien taken other, even more risqué pictures? And her mother...what insanity had persuaded her to risk her job by trashing her employer to a tabloid journalist? Poppy's soft full mouth downcurved and her shoulders slumped as she climbed back on her bike. Unfortunately Poppy knew exactly why her mother might have been so foolish: Jasmine Arnold was an alcoholic.

Poppy had once got her mother to an AA meeting and it had done her good but she had never managed to get the older woman back to a second. Instead, Jasmine just drank herself insensible every day while Poppy struggled to do her mother's job for her as well as doing her own. What else could she do when the very roof over their heads was dependent on Jasmine's continuing employment? And after all, wasn't it *her* fault that her mother had sunk so low before Poppy realised how bad things had got in her own home and had finally come back to live with her family again?

It was very fortunate that Gaetano only visited the house once or twice a year. But then Gaetano was a city boy through and through and a beautiful Georgian country house an inconvenient distance from London was of little use or interest to him. Had he been a more regular visitor she would never have been able to conceal her mother's condition for so long.

Poppy pumped the bike pedals hard to get up the hill before careening at speed into the driveway of Woodfield Hall. The beautiful house had been the Leonetti family home in England since the eighteenth century when the family had first come over from Venice to set up as glorified moneylenders. And if there was one thing that family were good at it, it was making pots and pots of money, Poppy reflected ruefully, shying away from the challenge of thinking about Gaetano in an any more personal way.

She and Gaetano might have virtually grown

up in the same household but it would be an out-right lie to suggest that they were ever in any way friendly. After all, Gaetano was six years older and had spent most of his time in posh board-ing schools.

But Poppy knew that Gaetano would go crazy about the publication of those photos. He was fanatical about his privacy and if his idea of fun was a sex party, she could perfectly under-stand why! Her spirits sank at the prospect of the trouble looming ahead. No matter how hard she worked life never seemed to get any easier and there always seemed to be another crisis waiting to erupt round the next corner. Yet how could she look after her mother and her brother when their own survival instincts appeared to be so poor?

The Arnold family lived in a flat that had been converted from part of the original stable block at the hall. Jasmine Arnold, a tall skinny redhead in her late forties, was sitting at the kitchen table when her daughter walked in.

Poppy slapped down the paper on the table.

'Mum? Were you out of your mind when you talked to a journalist about that party?' she demanded, before opening the back door and yelling her brother's name at the top of her voice.

Damien emerged from one of the garages, wiping oil stains off his hands with a dirty cloth. 'Where's the fire?' he asked irritably as his sister moved forward to greet him.

'You gave the photos you took at that party to a journalist?' his sister challenged in disbelief.

'No, I didn't,' her kid brother countered. 'Mum knew they were on my phone and she handed them over. She sold them. Got a pile of cash for them and the interview.'

Poppy was even more appalled. She could have excused stupidity or careless speech to the wrong person but she was genuinely shocked that her mother had taken money in return for her disloyalty to her employer.

Damien groaned at the expression on his sister's face. 'Poppy…you should know by now that Mum would do anything to get the money to buy her next drink,' he pointed out heavily. 'I told her not to hand over the photos or talk to the guy but she wouldn't listen to me—'

'Why didn't you tell me what she'd done?'

'What could you do about it? I hoped that maybe the photos wouldn't be used or that, if they were, nobody of any importance would see them,' Damien admitted. 'I doubt if Gaetano sits down to read every silly story that's written about him…I mean, he's never out of the papers!'

'But if you're wrong, Mum will be sacked and we'll be kicked out of the flat.'

Damien wasn't the type to worry about what might never happen and he said wryly, 'Let's hope I'm not wrong.'

But Poppy took after her late father and she was a worrier. It was hard to credit that it was only a few years since the Arnolds had been a secure and happy family of four. Her father had been the gardener at Woodfield Hall and her mother the housekeeper. At twenty years of age, Poppy had been two years into her training at nursing school and Damien had just completed his apprenticeship as a car mechanic. And then without any warning at all their much-loved father had dropped dead and all their lives had been shattered by that cruelly sudden bereavement.

Poppy had taken time out from her course to try and help her mother through the worst of her grief and then she had returned to her studies. Unhappily and without her knowledge, things had gone badly wrong at that point. Her mother had gone off the rails and Damien had been unable to cope with what was happening in his home. Her brother had then got in with the wrong crowd and had ended up in prison. That was when Poppy had finally come home to find her mother sunk in depression and drinking heavily. Poppy had taken a leave of absence from her course, hoping, indeed expecting, that her mother would soon pull round again. Unfortunately that hadn't happened. Although Jasmine was still drinking, Poppy's one consolation was that, after earning early release from prison with his good behaviour, her little brother had got his act together again. Sadly, however, Damien's criminal record had made it impossible for him to get a job.

Poppy still felt horribly guilty about the fact that she had left her kid brother to deal with her deeply troubled mother. Intent on pursuing her chosen career and being the first Arnold female in generations *not* to earn her living by serving the Leonettis, she had been selfish and thoughtless and she had been trying to make up for that mistake ever since.

When she returned to the flat her mother had locked herself in her bedroom. Poppy suppressed a sigh and dug out her work kit and rubber gloves to cross the courtyard and enter the hall. She turned out different rooms of the big house every week, dusting and vacuuming and scrubbing. It was deeply ironic that she had been so set against working for the Leonettis when she was a teenager but had ended up doing it anyway even if it was unofficial. Evenings she served drinks in the local pub. There wasn't time in her life for agonising when there was always a job needing to be done.

Disturbingly however she couldn't get Gaetano Leonetti out of her mind. He was the one and only boy she had ever hated but also the only one she had ever loved. What did that say about her? Self-evidently, that at the age of sixteen she had been really stupid to imagine for one moment that she could ever have any kind of a personal relationship with the posh, privileged scion of the Leonetti family. The wounding demeaning words that Gaetano had shot at her then were still burned into her bones like the scars of an old breakage.

'*I don't mess around with staff,*' he had said, emphasising the fact that they were not equals and that he would always inhabit a different stratum of society.

'*Stop coming on to me, Poppy. You're acting like a slapper.*' Oh, how she had cringed at that reading of her behaviour when in truth she had merely been too young and inexperienced to know how to be subtle about spelling out the fact that should he be interested, she was available.

'You're a short, curvy redhead. You could never be my type.'

It was seven years since that humiliating exchange had taken place and apart from one final demeaning encounter she had not seen Gaetano since, having always gone out of her way to avoid him whenever he was expected at the hall. So, he didn't know that she had slimmed down and shot up inches in height, wouldn't much care either, she reckoned with wry amusement. After all, Gaetano went for very beautiful and sophisticated ladies in designer clothes. Although the one who had thrown that shockingly wild party had not been much of a lady in the original sense of the word.

Having put in her hours at the hall in the ongoing challenge to ensure that it was always well prepared for a visit that could come at very short notice, Poppy went back home to get changed for her bar work. Jasmine was out for the count on her bed, an empty bottle of cheap wine lying beside her. Studying her slumped figure, Poppy suppressed a sigh, recalling the busy, lively and caring woman her mother had once been. Alcohol had stolen all that from her. Jasmine needed specialised help and rehabilitation but there wasn't even counselling available locally and Poppy had no hope of ever acquiring sufficient cash to pay for private treatment for the older woman.

Poppy put on the Goth clothes that she had first donned like a mask to hide behind when she was a bullied teenager. She had been picked on in school for being a little overweight and red-haired. Heck, she had even been bullied for being 'posh' although her family lived in the hall's servant accommodation. Since then, although she no longer dyed her hair or painted her nails black, she had come to enjoy a touch of individuality in her wardrobe and had maintained the basic style. She had lost a lot of weight since she started working two jobs and she was convinced that her Goth-style clothes did a good job of disguising her skinniness. For work she had teamed a dark red net flirty skirt with a fitted black jersey rock print top. The outfit hugged her small full breasts, enhanced her waist and accentuated the length of her legs.

At the end of her shift in the busy bar that was paired with a popular restaurant, Poppy pulled on her coat and waited outside for Damien to show up on his motorbike.

'Gaetano Leonetti arrived in a helicopter this evening,' her brother delivered curtly. 'He demanded to see Mum but she was out of it and I had to pretend she was sick. He handed over these envelopes for her and I opened them once he'd gone. Mum's being sacked and we have a month's notice to move out of the flat.'

An anguished moan of dismay at those twin blows parted Poppy's lips.

'I guess he did see that newspaper.' Damien grimaced. 'He certainly hasn't wasted any time booting us out.'

'Can we blame him for that?' Poppy asked even

though her heart was sinking to the soles of her shoes. Where would they go? How would they live? They had no rainy-day account for emergencies. Her mother drank her salary and Damien was on benefits.

But Poppy was a fighter, always had been, always would be. She took after her father more than her mother. She was good at picking herself up when things went wrong. Her mother, however, had never fully recovered from the stillbirth she had suffered the year before Poppy's father had died. Those two terrible calamities coming so close together had knocked her mother's feet from under her and she had never really got up again. Poppy swallowed hard as she climbed onto the bike and gripped her brother's waist. She could still remember her mother's absolute joy at that unexpected late pregnancy, which in the end had become a source of so much grief and loss.

As the bike rolled past the hall Poppy saw the light showing through the front window of the library and tensed. Gaetano was staying over for the night?

'Yeah, he's still here,' Damien confirmed as he put his bike away. 'So what?'

'I'm going to speak to him—'

'What's the point?' her brother asked in a tone of defeat. 'Why should he care?'

But Gaetano *did* have a heart, Poppy thought in desperation. At least he had had a heart at the age of thirteen when his father had run over his dog and killed it. She had seen the tears in Gaetano's eyes and she had been crying too. Dino had been as much her dog as his because Dino had hung around with her when Gaetano was away at school, not that he had probably ever realised that. Dino had never been replaced and when she had asked why not in the innocent way of a child, Gaetano had simply said flatly, 'Dogs die.'

And she had been too young to really understand that outlook, that raising of the barriers against the threat of being hurt again. She had seen no tears in his remarkable eyes at his father's funeral but he had been almost as devastated as his grandfather when his grandmother passed away. But then the older couple had been more his parents than his real parents had. Within a year of becoming a widow, his mother had re-married and moved to Florida without her son.

Poppy breathed in deep as she marched round the side of the big house with Damien chasing in her wake.

'It's almost midnight!' he hissed. 'You can't go calling on him now!'

'If I wait until tomorrow I'll lose my nerve,' she said truthfully.

Damien hung back in the shadows, watching as she rang the doorbell and waited, her hands dug in the pockets of her faux-leather flying jacket. A voice sounded somewhere close by and she flinched in surprise, turning her head as a man in a suit talking into a mobile phone walked to-wards her in the moonlight.

'I'm security, Miss Arnold,' he said quietly. 'I was telling Mr Leonetti who was at the door.'

Poppy suppressed a rude word. She had forgotten the tight security with which the Leonetti family surrounded themselves. Of course, calling in on Gaetano late at night wouldn't go unquestioned.

'I want to see your boss,' she declared.

The security man was talking Italian into the phone and she couldn't follow a word of what he was saying. When the man frowned, she knew he was about to deliver a negative and she moved off the step and snapped, 'I *have* to see Gaetano! It's really important.'

Somewhere someone made a decision and a moment later there was the sound of heavy bolts being drawn back to open the massive front door. Another security man nodded acknowledgement and stood back for her entrance into the marble-floored hall with its perfect proportions and priceless paintings. A trickle of perspiration ran down between her taut shoulder blades and she straightened her spine in defiance of it although she was already shrinking at the challenge of what she would have to tell Gaetano. At this juncture, coming clean was her sole option.

Poppy Arnold? Gaetano's brain had conjured up several time-faded images. Poppy as a little girl paddling at the lake edge in spite of his warnings; Poppy sobbing over Dino with all the drama of her class and no thought of restraint; Poppy looking at him as if he might imminently walk on water when she was about fifteen, a scrutiny that had become considerably less innocent and entertaining a year later. And finally, Poppy, a taunting sensual smile tilting her lips as she sidled out of the shrubbery closely followed by a young estate worker, both of them engaged in righting their rumpled, grass-stained clothing.

Bearing in mind the number of years the Arnold family had worked for his own, he felt that it was only fair that he at least saw Poppy and listened to what she had to say in her mother's defence. He hadn't, however, thought about Poppy in years. Did she still live with her family? He was surprised, having always assumed Poppy would flee country life and the type of employment she had soundly trounced as being next door to indentured servitude in the modern world. Touching a respectful forelock had held no appeal whatsoever for outspoken, rebellious Poppy, he acknowledged wryly. How much had she changed? Was she working for him now somewhere on the pay roll? His ebony brows drew together in a frown at his ignorance as he lounged back against the edge of the library desk and awaited her appearance.

The tap-tap of high heels sounded in the corridor and the door opened to reveal legs that could have rivalled a Vegas showgirl's toned and perfect pins. Disconcerted by that startlingly unexpected and carnal thought, Gaetano ripped his attention from those incredibly long shapely legs and whipped it up to her face, only to receive another jolt. Time had transformed Poppy

Arnold into a tall, dazzling redhead. He was staring but he couldn't help it while his shrewd brain was engaged in ticking off familiarities and changes. The bright green eyes were unaltered but the rounded face had fined down to an exquisite heart shape to frame slanting cheekbones, a dainty little nose and a mouth lush and pink enough to star in any male fantasy. The pulse at Gaetano's groin throbbed and he straightened, flicking his jacket closed to conceal his physical reaction while thinking that Poppy might well get the last laugh after all because the ugly duckling he had once rejected had become a swan.

'Mr Leonetti,' she said as politely as though they had never met before.

'Gaetano, please,' he countered wryly, seeing no reason to stand on ceremony with her. 'We have known each other since childhood.'

'I don't think I ever *knew* you,' Poppy said frankly, studying him with bemused concentration.

She had expected to notice unappetising

changes in Gaetano. After all, he was almost thirty years old now and lived a deskbound, self-indulgent and, by all accounts, *decadent* life. By this stage he should have been showing some physical fallout from that lifestyle. But there was no hint of portliness in his very tall, powerfully built frame and certainly no jowls to mar the perfection of his strong, stubbled jaw line. And his dense blue-black curly hair was as plentiful as ever.

An electrifying silence enclosed them and Poppy stepped restively off one foot onto the other, her slender figure tense as a drawn bow string while she studied him. Taller and broader than he had been, he was even more gorgeous than he had been seven years earlier when she had fallen for him like a ton of bricks. Silly, silly girl that she had been, she conceded ruefully, but there was no denying that even then she had had good taste because Gaetano was stunning in the way so very few men were. A tiny flicker in her pelvis made her press her thighs together, warmth flushing over her skin. His dark eyes, set below black straight brows, were locked to her with an intensity that made her inwardly squirm. He had eyes with incredibly long thick lashes, she was recalling dizzily, so dark and noticeable in their volume that she had once suspected him of wearing guy liner like some of the boys she had known back then.

'Do you still live here with your mother and brother?' Gaetano enquired.

'Yes,' Poppy admitted, fighting to banish the fog that had briefly closed round her brain. 'You're probably wondering why I've come to see you at this hour. I'm a bartender at the Flying Horseman down the road and I've only just finished my shift.'

Gaetano was pleasantly surprised that she had contrived to speak two entire sentences without spluttering the profanities which had laced her speech seven years earlier. Of course, right now she was probably watching her every word with him, he reasoned. A bartender? He supposed it explained the outfit, which looked as though it would be more at home in a nightclub.

'I saw the newspaper article,' she added. 'Obviously you want to sack my mother for talking about the party and selling those photos. I'm not denying that you have good reason to do that.'

'Where did the photos come from?' Gaetano asked curiously. 'Who took them?'

Poppy winced. 'One of the guests invited my brother to join the party when she saw him outside directing cars. He did what I imagine most young men would do when they see half-naked women—he took pictures on his phone. I'm not excusing him but he didn't sell those photos... It was my mother who took his phone and did that—'

'I assume I'll see your mother in person tomorrow before I leave. But I'll ask you now. My family has always treated your mother well. Why did she *do* it?'

Poppy breathed in deep and lifted her chin, bracing herself for what she had to say. 'My mother's an alcoholic, Gaetano. They offered her money and that was all it took. All she was thinking about was probably how she would buy her next bottle of booze. I'm afraid she can't see beyond that right now.'

Taken aback, Gaetano frowned. He had not been prepared for that revelation. It did not make a difference to his attitude though. Disloyalty was not a trait he could overlook in an employee. 'Your mother must be a functioning alcoholic, then,' he assumed. 'Because the house appears to be in good order.'

'No, she's not functioning.' Poppy sighed, her soft mouth tightening. 'I've been covering up for her for more than a year. I've been looking after this place.'

His lean, darkly handsome features tightened. 'In other words there has been a concentrated campaign to deceive me as to what was going on here,' he condemned with a sudden harshness that dismayed her. 'At any time you could have approached me and asked for my understanding and even my help—yet you chose not to do so. I have no tolerance for deception, Poppy. This meeting is at an end.'

A hundred different thoughts flashing through her mind, Poppy stared at him, her heart beating very fast with nerves and consternation. 'But—'

'No extenuating circumstances allowed or invited,' Gaetano cut in with derision. 'I have heard all I need to hear from you and there is nothing more to say. *Leave*.'

CHAPTER TWO

POPPY TOOK A sudden step forward. 'Don't speak to me like that!' she warned Gaetano angrily.

'I can speak to you whatever way I like. I'm in my own home and it seems that you are one of my employees.'

'No, I'm not!' Poppy contradicted with unashamed satisfaction. 'I donated my services free for my mother's sake!'

'Let's not make it sound as if you dug ditches,' Gaetano fired back impatiently. 'As I'm so rarely here there can't be that much work concerned in keeping the house presentable.'

'I think you'd be surprised by how much work is involved in a place this size!' Poppy snapped back firely.

Anger made her green eyes shine blue-green

like a peacock feather, Gaetano noted. 'I'm really not interested,' he said drily. 'And if you donated your services free that was downright stupid, not praiseworthy.'

Poppy almost stamped an enraged foot. 'I'm not stupid. How dare you say that? I could hardly charge you for the work my mother was already being paid to do, could I?'

Gaetano shrugged a broad shoulder, watching her tongue flick out to moisten her red-lipsticked mouth, imagining her doing other much dirtier things with it and then tensing with exquisite discomfort as arousal coursed feverishly through his lower body. She was sexy, smoulderingly so, he acknowledged grimly. 'I'm sure you're versatile enough to have found some way round that problem.'

'But not dishonest enough to do so,' Poppy proclaimed with pride. 'Mum was being paid for the job and it was done, so on that score you have no grounds for complaint.'

'I don't?' An ebony brow lifted in challenge.

'An alcoholic has been left in charge of the house-hold accounts?'

'Oh, no, that's not been happening,' Poppy has-tened to reassure him. 'Mum no longer has ac-cess to the household cash. I made sure of that early on.'

'Then how have the bills been paid?'

Poppy compressed her lips as she registered that he truly did not have a clue how his own household had worked for years. 'I paid them. I've been taking care of the accounts here since Dad died.'

'But you're not authorised!' Gaetano slammed back at her distrustfully.

'Neither was my father but he took care of them for a long time.'

Gaetano's frown grew even darker. 'Your fa-ther had access as well? What the hell?'

'Oh, for goodness' sake, are you always this rigid?' Poppy groaned in disbelief. 'Mum never had a head for figures. Dad always did the ac-counts for her. Your grandmother knew. Whenever your grandmother had a query about the accounts she had to wait until Mum had asked Dad for the answer. It wasn't a secret back then.'

'And how am I supposed to trust you with substantial sums of money when your brother was recently in prison for theft?' Gaetano demanded sharply. 'My accountants will check the accounts and, believe me, if there are any discrepancies I will be bringing in the police.'

Having paled when he threw his knowledge of Damien's conviction at her, Poppy stood very straight and still, her facial muscles tight with self-control. 'Damien got involved with a gang of car thieves but he didn't actually *steal* any of the cars. He's the mechanic who worked on the stolen vehicles before they were shipped abroad to be sold.'

'What a very fine distinction!' Gaetano derided, unimpressed.

Poppy raised her head high, green eyes flashing defiance like sparks. 'You get your accountants in to check the books. There won't be any discrepancies,' she fired back with pride. 'And don't be snide about my brother.'

'I wasn't being snide.'

'You were being snide from the pinnacle of your rich, privileged, feather-bedded life. Damien broke the law and he was punished for it,' Poppy told him. 'He's paid his dues and he's learned his lesson. Maybe you've never made any mistakes, Gaetano?'

'My mistake was in allowing that party to be held here!' Gaetano slung back at her grittily. 'And don't drag my background or my wealth into this conversation. It's unfair—'

'Then don't be so superior!' Poppy advised. 'But maybe you can't help being the way you are.'

'Do you really think hurling insults at me is likely to further your cause?'

'You haven't even given me the chance to tell you what my cause is,' she pointed out. 'You're so argumentative, Gaetano!'

'*I'm*...argumentative?' Gaetano carolled in disbelief.

'I want you to give Mum another chance,' Poppy admitted doggedly. 'I know you're not feeling very generous. I know that having your kinky party preferences splashed all over the media has to have been embarrassing for you—'

'I do not have kinky preferences—'

'It's none of my business whether you do or not!' Poppy riposted. 'I'm not being judgemental.'

'How very generous of you in the circumstances,' Gaetano murmured icily.

'And if you're not being argumentative, you're being sarcastic!' Poppy flared back at him with raw resentment. 'Can you even *try* listening to me?'

'If you could try to refrain from commenting about my preferences, kinky or otherwise,' Gaetano advised flatly.

'May I take my shoes off?' she asked him abruptly. 'I've been standing all night and my feet are killing me!'

Gaetano shifted an impatient hand. 'Take them

off. Say what you have to say and then go. I'm bored with this.'

'You're so kind and encouraging,' Poppy replied in a honeyed tone of stinging sweetness as she removed her shoes and dropped several crucial inches in height, unsettled by the reality that, although she was five feet eight inches tall, he had a good six inches on her and now towered over her in a manner she instinctively disliked.

As she flexed those incredible long legs sheathed in black lace, Gaetano watched, admiring her long toned calves, neat little knees and long slender thighs. A flash of white inner thigh as she bent in that short skirt and her small full breasts shifting unbound below the clinging top sent his temperature rocketing and made his teeth grit. Was she teasing him deliberately? Was the provocative outfit a considered invitation? What woman dressed like that came to see a man at midnight with clean intentions?

'Talk, Poppy,' he urged very drily, infuriated at the way his brain was rebelling against his usual rational control and concentration to stray in directions he was determined not to travel.

'Mum has had it tough the last few years—'

Gaetano held up a silencing hand. 'I know about the stillbirth and of course your father's death and I'm heartily sorry for the woman, but those misfortunes don't excuse what's been happening here.'

'Mum needs help, not judgement, Gaetano,' Poppy argued shakily.

'I'm her employer, not her family and not a therapist,' Gaetano pointed out calmly. 'She's not my responsibility.'

In a more hesitant voice, Poppy added, 'Your grandfather always said we were one big family here.'

'Please don't tell me that you fell for that old chestnut. My grandfather is an old-fashioned man who likes the sound of such sentiments but somehow I don't think he'd be any more compassionate than I am when it comes to the security of his home. Leaving an untrustworthy and unstable alcoholic in charge here would be complete madness,' he stated coolly.

'Yes, but…you could give Mum's job to me,' Poppy reasoned in a desperate rush. 'I've been doing it to your satisfaction for months, so you've actually had a free trial. That way we could stay on in the flat and you wouldn't have to look for someone new.'

Discomfiture made Gaetano tense. 'You never wanted to do domestic work…I'm well aware of that.'

'We all have to do things we don't want to do, particularly when it comes to looking out for family,' Poppy argued with feeling. 'After Dad died I went back to my nursing course and left Damien looking after Mum. He couldn't cope. He didn't tell me how bad things had got here and because of that he got into trouble. Mum is my responsibility and I turned my back on her when she needed me most.'

Gaetano, who was unsurprised that she had sought a career outside domestic service, thought she had a ridiculously overactive conscience. 'It wouldn't work, Poppy. I'm sorry. I wish you well and I'm sorry I can't help.'

'*Won't* help,' she slotted in curtly.

'You're not my idea of a housekeeper. It's best that you make a new start somewhere else with your family,' he declared.

No, he definitely didn't want Poppy with her incredibly alluring legs in his house, even though he didn't visit it very often. She would be a dangerous temptation and he was determined that he would never go there. *Never muck around with staff* was a maxim etched in stone in Gaetano's personal commandments. When a former PA had thrown herself at him one evening early in his career he had slept with her. For him it had been a one-night stand on a business trip and nothing more, but she had been far more ambitious and it had ended messily, teaching him that professional relationships should never cross the boundaries into intimacy.

'It's not that easy to make a new start,' Poppy

told him tightly. 'I'm the only one out of the three of us with a job and if I have to move I'll lose that.'

Gaetano expelled his breath on an impatient hiss. 'Poppy…I am not going to apologise for the fact that your mother breached her employment contract and plunged me into a scandal. You cannot lay her problems at my door. I have every sympathy for your position and, out of consideration for the years that your family worked here and did an excellent job, I will make a substantial final payment—'

'Oh, keep your blasted conscience money!' Poppy flung at him, suddenly losing her temper, her fierce pride stung by his attitude. He thought that she and her mother and her brother were a sad bunch of losers and he was so keen to get them off his property that he was prepared to pay more for the privilege. 'I don't want anything from you. I won't *take* anything more from you!'

'Losing your temper is a very bad idea in a situation like this,' he breathed irritably as she bent down to scoop up her shoes and turned on her heel, her short skirt flaring round her pert behind.

Poppy turned her head, green eyes gleaming like polished jewels. 'It's the only thing I've got left to lose,' she contradicted squarely.

Gaetano threw up his hands in a gesture of frustration. 'Then why the hell are you *doing* it? Put yourself first and leave your family to sort out their own problems!'

'Is that what the ruthless, callous banker would do to save his own skin?' Poppy asked scornfully as she reached the door. 'Mum and Damien are my family and, yes, they're very different from me. I take after Dad and I'm strong. They're not. They crumble in a crisis. Does that mean I love them any less? No, it doesn't. In fact it probably means I love them *more*. I love them warts and all and as long as there's breath in my body I'll look after them to the best of my ability.'

Gaetano was stunned into silence by her emotive words. He couldn't imagine loving anyone like that. His parents had been both been weak and fallible in their different ways. His father had chased thrills and his mother had chased money and Gaetano had only learned to despise them for their shallow characters. His parents had not had the capacity to love him and once he had got old enough to understand that he had stopped loving them, ultimately recognising that only his grand-parents genuinely cared about him and his well-being. For that reason, the concept of continuing to blindly love seriously flawed personalities and still feel a duty of care towards them genuinely shocked Gaetano, who was infinitely more discerning and demanding of those closest to him. He had seen Poppy Arnold's strength and he admired it, but he thought she was a complete fool to allow her wants and wishes to be handicapped by the double burden of a drunken mother and a pretty useless kid brother.

He went for a shower, still mulling over the encounter with a feeling of amazement that grew rather than dwindled. Rodolfo Leonetti would have been hugely impressed by Poppy's speech, he acknowledged grimly. His grandfather, after all, had wasted years striving to advise and support his feckless son and his frivolous daughter-in-law. Rodolfo had overlooked their faults and had compassionately made the best of a bad situation. Gaetano, however, was much tougher than the older man, less patient, less forgiving, less sympathetic. Was that a flaw in him? he wondered for the very first time.

Thinking of how much Rodolfo would have applauded Poppy's family loyalty, Gaetano reflected equally on her flaws that Rodolfo would have cringed from. Her background was dreadful, the family unpalatable. Mother an alcoholic? Brother a convicted criminal? Poppy's provocative clothing and use of bad language? And yet wasn't Poppy Arnold an ordinary girl of the type Rodolfo had always contended would make his grandson a perfect wife?

Having towelled himself dry, Gaetano got into bed naked and lay there, lost in thought. A sudden laugh escaped him as he momentarily allowed himself to imagine his grandfather's horror if he were to produce a young woman like Poppy as his future wife. Rodolfo was much more of a snob than he would ever be prepared to admit and it was hardly surprising that he should be for the Leonettis had been a family of great wealth and power for hundreds of years. Yet the same man had risked disinheritance when he had married a fisherman's daughter against his family's wishes. Gaetano couldn't imagine that kind of love. He felt no need for that sort of excessive emotion in his life. In fact the very idea of it terrified him and always had.

He didn't want to get married. Maybe by the time he was in his forties he would have mellowed a little and would feel the need to settle down with a companion. At some point too he should have a child to continue the family line. He flinched from the concept, remembering his father's temper tantrums and his mother's tears and nagging whines. Marriage had a bad image with him. Why couldn't Rodolfo understand and accept that reality? He was just too young for settling down but not too young to take over as CEO of the bank.

The germ of an idea occurred to Gaetano and struck him as weird, so he discarded it, only to take it out again a few minutes later and examine it in greater depth. Suppose he quite deliberately produced a fiancée whom his grandfather would deem wrong for him? In that scenario nobody would be the slightest bit surprised when the engagement was broken off again and Rodolfo would be relieved rather than disappointed. He would see that Gaetano had made an effort to commit to a woman and honour that change accordingly by giving his grandson breathing space for quite some time afterwards. A fake incompatible fiancée could get him off the hook...

In the moonlight piercing the curtains, Gaetano's lean, darkly handsome features were beginning to form a shadowy smile. Pick an ordinary girl and she would naturally have to be beautiful if his grandfather was to be convinced that his fastidious grandson had fallen for her. Pick a beautiful ordinary girl guaranteed to be an embarrassment in public. Poppy could drop all the profanities she liked, dress like a hooker and tell everybody about her sordid family problems. He wouldn't even have to prime her to fail in his exclusive world. It was a given that she would be so out of her depth that she would automatically do so.

A sliver of the conscience that Gaetano rarely listened to slunk out to suggest that it would be a little cruel to subject Poppy to such an ordeal merely for the sake of initially satisfying and then hopefully changing his grandfather's expectations. But then it wouldn't be a real engagement. She would know from the outset that she was faking it and she would be handsomely paid for her role. Nor would she need to know that he was expecting, no, *depending* on her to be a social embarrassment to get him out of the engagement again. It would sort of be like *Pygmalion* in reverse, he reasoned with quiet satisfaction. Pick an ordinary girl, who was an extraordinary beauty and extremely outspoken and hot-tempered... She would be absolutely perfect for his purposes because she would be an accident waiting to happen.

Poppy barely slept that night. Gaetano had said and done nothing unexpected. Of course he wanted them off his fancy property, out of sight and out of mind! His incredulous attitude to her attachment to her family had appalled her though. And where were they going to go? And how would they live when they got there? She would have to throw them on the tender mercies of the social services. My goodness, would they end up living in one of those homeless hostels? Eating out of a food bank?

She got up early as usual, relishing that quiet time of day before her mother or her brother stirred. Even better it was a sunny morning and she took her coffee out to the tiny square of garden at the back of the building that was her favourite place in the world. Making plants flourish, simply growing things, gave her great pleasure.

A riot of flowers in pots ornamented the tiny paved area with its home-made bench seat that was more than a little rickety. However, her Dad had made that bench and she would never part with it. With the clear blue sky above and birds singing in the trees nearby, she felt guilty for feeling so stressed and unhappy. When she had been a little girl working by her father's side she had wanted to be a gardener. Assuming that that would inevitably mean one day working for the Leonettis, she had changed her mind, ignorant of the reality that there were a host of training courses and jobs in the horticultural world far from Woodfield Hall that she could have aspired to. Well, so much for her planned escape, she thought heavily. Now that they were being evicted, she didn't want to leave.

'Miss Arnold?' One of Gaetano's security men

looked over the fence at her. 'Mr Leonetti wants to see you.'

Poppy leapt upright. Had he had second thoughts about his decision? She smoothed down the thin jacket she wore over a black gothic dress. She had expected Gaetano to demand to see her mother again and she had dressed up in her equivalent of armour to tell him that her mother would be incapable of even speaking to him until midday. She walked round the side of the building and headed towards the house.

'Mr Leonetti is waiting for you at the helicopter.'

So, he was planning to toss a two-minute speech at her and depart, Poppy gathered ruefully. It didn't sound as though he'd had a change of heart, did it? She followed the path to the helipad at the far side of the hall, identifying Gaetano as the taller man in the small clump of waiting males who included the pilot and Gaetano's security staff. In a pale grey exquisitely tailored designer suit, his arrogant dark head held high,

Gaetano looked like a king, and as she moved towards him he stood there much like a king waiting for her to come to him. So, what was new? Gaetano Leonetti didn't have a humble bone in his magnificent body. No, no, less of the magnificent, she scolded herself angrily. No way was she going to look admiringly at the male making her and her family homeless, even if he did have just cause!

'Good morning, Poppy,' Gaetano drawled, smooth as glass, scanning her appearance in the form-fitting black dress that brushed her knees and what appeared to be combat boots with keen appreciation. The jacket looked as if it belonged to a circus ringmaster and he almost smiled at the prospect of his grandfather's disquiet. Clearly, Poppy always dressed strangely and he could certainly work with that eccentricity. In fact the more eccentricities, the better. And she looked amazingly well in that weird outfit with her freckle-free skin like whipped cream and her hair tumbling in silky bronzed ringlets round her slight shoulders, highlighting her alluring face.

He was not attracted to her, he told himself resolutely. He could appreciate a woman's looks without wanting to bed her. He wasn't that basic in his tastes, was he? The incipient throb of a hard-on, however, hinted that he might be a great deal more basic than he wanted to believe. Of course that was acceptable too, Gaetano conceded shrewdly. Rodolfo was no fool and would soon notice any apparent lack of sexual chemistry.

Poppy thought about faking a posh accent like his and abandoned the idea because Gaetano would be slow to see the joke, if he saw one at all. 'Morning,' she said lazily in her usual abbreviated style.

'We're going out for breakfast since there's no food in the house,' Gaetano murmured huskily.

Poppy blinked, catching the flick of censure but too caught up in the positive purr of his deep, slightly accented drawl, which was sending a peculiar little shiver down her taut spine. *'We?'* she queried belatedly, green eyes opening very wide.

Gaetano noted that her pupils were surrounded by a ring of tawny brown that merely emphasised the bright green of her eyes and said quietly, 'I have a proposition I want to discuss with you.'

'A proposition?' she questioned with a frown.

'Breakfast,' Gaetano reminded her and he bent to plant his hands to her hips and swing her up into the helicopter before she could even guess his intention.

'For breakfast we get into a helicopter?' Poppy framed in bewilderment.

'We're going to a hotel.'

A proposition? Her mind was blank as to what possible suggestions he might be able to put to her in her family's current predicament and, although she was far from entertained by his virtual kidnapping, she knew she was in no position to tell him to get lost. Even so, Poppy would very much have enjoyed telling Gaetano to get lost. His innate dominant traits set her teeth on edge, not to mention the manner in which he simply assumed that everyone around him would jump to do his bidding without argument. And he was probably right in that assumption, she thought resentfully. He had money, power and influence and she had none of those things.

The craft was so noisy that there was no possibility of conversation during the short flight. Poppy peered down without surprise as the biggest, flashiest country-house hotel in the area appeared below them. Only the very best would do for Gaetano, she thought in exasperation, wishing she'd had some warning of his plan. She had no make-up on and not even a comb with her and wasn't best pleased to find herself about to enter a very snooty five-star establishment where everyone else, including her host, would be groomed to perfection. And here she was wearing combat boots ready to cycle to the shop for a newspaper.

Deliberately avoiding Gaetano's extended arms, Poppy jumped down onto the grass. 'You could've warned me about where we were going...I'm not dressed—'

Gaetano dealt her a slow-burning smile, dark golden eyes brilliant in the sunshine. 'You look fabulous.'

Her mouth ran dry and suddenly she needed a deep breath but somehow couldn't get sufficient oxygen into her lungs. That shockingly appealing smile...when he had never smiled at her before. Gaetano was as stingy as a miser with his smiles. Why *was* he suddenly smiling at her? What did he want? What had changed? And why was he telling her that she looked *fabulous*? Especially when his raised-brow appraisal as she'd approached him at the helipad had told her that he knew about as much about her style as she knew about high finance.

At the door of the hotel they were greeted by the manager as though they were royalty and ushered to the 'Orangery' where Gaetano was assured that they would not be disturbed. Had there been a chaise longue, Poppy would have flopped down on it like a Victorian maiden and would have asked Gaetano if he was planning a seduction just to annoy him. But if he had a proposition that might ease her family's current situation she was more than willing to listen without making cheeky comments, she told herself. Unfortunately, her tongue often ran ahead of her brain, especially around Gaetano, who didn't have to do much to infuriate her.

CHAPTER THREE

'THAT...ER...' POPPY hastily revised the word she had been about to employ for a more tactful one. 'That remark you made about there being no food in the house... We didn't know you were coming to the hall,' she reminded him.

Gaetano watched a waiter pull out a chair for Poppy before taking his own seat. Sunshine was cascading through the windows, transforming her bright hair into a fiery halo. She clutched her menu and ordered chocolate cereal and a hot-chocolate drink. He was astonished that the vast number of menu options had not tempted her into a more adventurous order.

'The hall is supposed to be kept fully stocked at all times,' Gaetano reminded her, having ordered.

Poppy shifted in her seat. 'But this way is much

more cost-effective, Gaetano. When I took over from Mum I was chucking out loads of fresh food every week and it hurt me to do it when there are people starving in this world. Until yesterday, someone always phoned to say you'd be visiting, so I cancelled the food deliveries… Oh, yes, and the flowers as well. I'm not into weekly flower arranging. I've saved you so much money,' she told him with pride.

'I don't need to save money. I expect the house to always be ready for use,' Gaetano countered drily.

Poppy gave him a pained look. 'But it's so wasteful…'

Gaetano shrugged. He had never thought about that aspect and did not see why he should consider it when he gave millions to charitable causes every year. Convenience and the ability to do as he liked, when he liked, and at short notice, were very important to him, because he rarely took time away from work. 'I'm not tight with cash,' he said wryly. 'If the house isn't prepared for immediate use, I can't visit whenever I take the notion.'

Poppy ripped open her small packet of cereal and poured it into the bowl provided. Ignoring the milk on offer, she began to eat the cereal dry with her fingers the way she always ate it. For a split second, Gaetano stared but said nothing. For that same split second she had felt slightly afraid that he might give her a slap across the knuckles for what he deemed to be poor table manners and she flushed pink with chagrin, determined not to alter her behaviour to kowtow to his different expectations. The rich were definitely different, she conceded ruefully.

'I will eat chocolate any way I can get it,' she confided nonetheless in partial apology. 'I don't like my cereal soggy. Now this proposition you mentioned…'

'My grandfather wants me to get married before I can become Chief Executive of the Leonetti Bank. As I don't want to get married, I believe a fake engagement would keep him happy in the short term. It will convince Rodolfo that I am moving in the right direction and assuage his fear that I'm incapable of settling down.'

'So, why are you telling me this?' Poppy asked him blankly.

'I want you to partner me in the fake engagement.' Gaetano lounged lithely back in his seat to study her reaction.

'You and me?' A peal of startled laughter erupted from Poppy's lush pink mouth beneath Gaetano's disconcerted gaze. 'You've got to be kidding. No one, but no one, would credit you and me as a couple!'

'Funny, you didn't see it as being that amusing when you were a teenager,' Gaetano derided softly.

'You are *such* a bastard!' Poppy sprang out of her chair, all pretence of cool abandoned as she stalked away from the table. She had never quite contrived to lose that tender, stinging sense of rejection and humiliation even though she knew she was being ridiculous. After all, she had been far too young and naïve for him as well as being the daughter of an employee, and for him to respond in any way, even had he wanted to, would have been inappropriate. But while her brain assured her of those facts, her visceral reaction was at another level.

A few weeks after his rebuff, the annual hall summer picnic had been held and Gaetano had put in his appearance with a girlfriend. Poppy had felt sick when she'd seen that shiny, beautifully dressed and classy girl who might have stepped straight out of a glossy modelling advertisement. She had seen how pathetic it had been to harbour even the smallest hope of ever attracting Gaetano's interest and as a result of that distress, that horrid feeling of unworthiness and mortification, she had plunged herself into a very unwise situation.

'Poppy…' Gaetano murmured wryly, wishing he had left that reminder of the past decently buried.

Poppy spun back to him, eyes wide and accusing. 'I was sixteen years old, for goodness' sake, and you were the only fanciable guy in my radius, so it's hardly surprising that I got a crush on you. It was hormones, nothing else. I wasn't mature enough to recognise that you were *totally* the wrong kind of guy for me—'

'Why?' Gaetano heard himself demand baldly, although no sooner had he asked than he was questioning why he had.

Poppy was equally surprised by that question. Her colour high, she stared at him, her clear green eyes luminescent in the sunlight. 'Why? Well, I've no doubt you're a great catch, being both rich and ridiculously good-looking,' she told him bluntly. 'You're a fiercely ambitious high achiever but you don't have heart. You're deadly serious and conventional too. We're complete opposites. People would only pair the two of us together in a comic book. Sorry, I hope I haven't insulted you in any way. That wasn't my intention.'

An almost imperceptible line of colour had fired along the exotic slant of Gaetano's spectacular cheekbones. He felt oddly as though he had been cut down to size and yet he couldn't fault what she had said because it was all true. There was an electric little silence. He glanced up from below his lashes and saw her standing there in the bright sunshine, her hair a blazing nimbus of red, bronze and gold in the light to give her the look of a fiery angel. Or in that severe black dress, a gothic angel of death? But it didn't matter because in that strange little instant when time stopped dead, Gaetano, rigid with raw arousal, wanted Poppy Arnold more than he had ever wanted any woman in his life and it gave him the chills like the scent of a good deal going bad. He breathed in slow and deep and looked away from her, battling to regain his logic and cool.

'I still want you to take on the role of playing my fake fiancée,' he breathed in a roughened undertone because just looking at her, drinking in that clear creamy skin, those luminous green eyes and that pink succulent mouth, was only making him harder than ever. 'Rodolfo always wanted me to choose an ordinary girl and you are the only one I know likely to fit the bill.'

Something in the way he was studying her made Poppy's mouth run dry and her breath hitch in her throat. She was suddenly aware of her body in a way she hadn't been aware of it in years. In fact, her physical reactions were knocking her right back to the discomfiting level of the infatuated teenager she had once been and that galled her, but the tight, prickling sensation in her breasts and the dampness between her thighs were uniquely memorable testaments to the temptation Gaetano provided. Falling for a very good-looking guy at sixteen and comparing every other man she had met afterwards to his detriment was not to be recommended as a life plan for any sensible woman, she reflected ruefully, ashamed of the fact that she couldn't treat Gaetano as casually as she treated other men.

'An ordinary girl?' she questioned with pleated brows, returning to the table to succumb to the allure of the melted marshmallows topping her hot chocolate. While she sipped, Gaetano filled her in on his grandfather's fond hopes for his future.

Poppy almost found herself laughing again. Gaetano would never genuinely *want* an ordinary girl and no ordinary girl would be able to cope with his essentially cold heart.

'So, why me?' she pressed.

'You're beautiful enough to convince him that I could be tempted by you—'

Guileless green eyes assailed his. 'Am I?'

'Yes, you're beautiful but, no, I'm not tempted,' Gaetano declared with stubborn conviction. 'When I say fake engagement I mean fake in *every* way. I will not be touching you.'

Poppy rolled her eyes. 'I wouldn't let you. I'm very, *very* picky, Gaetano.'

Gaetano resisted the urge to toss up the name of that young estate worker she had entertained in the shrubbery. Odd how he had never forgotten those details, he conceded, while recognising that such a crack would be cruelly inappropriate because she was as entitled to have enjoyed sex as any other woman. His perfect white teeth clenched together. He loathed the way Poppy somehow knocked him off-balance, tripping his mind into random thoughts, persuading his usually controlled tongue into making ill-advised remarks, turning him on when he didn't want to be turned on. Each and every one of those reactions offended Gaetano's pride in his strength of will.

'You've got to be wondering what would be in this arrangement for you,' Gaetano intoned quietly. 'Everything you want and need at present. Rehabilitation treatment for your mother, a fresh start somewhere, a new home for you all as security. I'll cover the cost of it all if you do this for me, *bella mia.*'

Straight off, Poppy saw that he was throwing her and her family a lifebelt when they were drowning and for that reason she didn't voice the refusal already brimming on her lips. Treatment for her mother. You couldn't put a price on such an offer. It was what she had dreamt about but knew she would never be able to afford.

'You've got to have a selfish bone somewhere in your body,' Gaetano declared. 'If you get your mother sorted out you can get your own life back and complete your nursing training, if that is still what you want to do.'

'I'm not sure I could be convincing as your ordinary-girl fiancée—'

'We'll cover that. Leave the worrying to me. I'm a skilled strategist,' Gaetano murmured, lush black lashes low over his beautiful dark golden eyes.

Her chest swelled as she dragged in a deep breath because really there was no decision to be made. Any attempt to sort out the mess her mother's life had become was worth a try. 'Then... where do I sign up?'

She had agreed. Having recognised that Poppy was pretty much between a rock and a hard place, Gaetano was not surprised by her immediate agreement. In his opinion she had much to gain and nothing at all to lose.

'So…er…' Poppy began uncertainly. 'You'll want me to dress up more…?'

A sudden wolfish smile flashed across Gaetano's lean, darkly handsome features. 'No, that's exactly what I don't want,' he assured her. 'Rodolfo would see straight through you trying to pretend to be something you're not. I don't want you to feel the need to change anything— just be yourself.'

'Myself…' Poppy repeated a tad dizzily as she collided with shimmering dark golden eyes fringed by those glorious spiky black lashes of his.

'Be yourself,' Gaetano stressed, severely disconcerting her because she had expected him to want to change everything about her. 'My grandfather, like me, respects individuality.'

Poppy wondered how it was then that, even in recent years, she had noticed from reading the papers, and catching a glimpse or two of past companions at the hall, Gaetano's women all seemed to be formed from the same identikit model. All were small, blonde and blue-eyed arm-clingers, who appeared to have no personality at all in his presence. The sort of women who simpered, hung on his every word and acted super-attentive to their man. No, Gaetano had definitely never struck her as a male likely to appreciate individuality.

'I would have another request,' she said daringly. 'My brother's a fully qualified mechanic. Find him a job.'

Gaetano frowned. 'He's an—'

'An ex-con. Yes, we are well aware of that, but he needs a proper job before he can hope to rebuild his life,' she pointed out. 'I'd be very grateful if there was anything you could do to help Damien.'

Gaetano's beautifully shaped mouth tightened. 'You drive a hard bargain. I'll make enquiries.'

Almost a full month after that breakfast, Poppy was sitting in the kitchen with her mother. Jasmine was studying her daughter and looking troubled, an expression that had become increasingly frequent on her face as she slowly emerged from the shrouding fog of alcoholic dependency and realised what had been happening in the world around her. Initial assessment followed by several sessions with trained counsellors and medication for her depression had brought about an improvement in Jasmine's state of mind. The older woman was trying not to drink, not doing very well so far but at least trying, something she had not even been prepared to contemplate just weeks earlier. This very afternoon Poppy and her mother were heading to London where Poppy would join Gaetano and take up her role as a fake fiancée while Jasmine embarked on a residential stay in a top-flight private clinic renowned for its success with patients.

'I just don't want to see you get hurt,' the older woman repeated, squeezing her daughter's hand. 'Gaetano is a real box of tricks. I appreciate his help, but I would never fully trust him. He's too clever and he hasn't got his granddad's humanity. I can't understand what's in this masquerade for Gaetano—'

'Climbing the career ladder at the bank—promotion. Seems that Rodolfo Leonetti is a real stick-in-the-mud about Gaetano still being single.' Poppy sighed, having already been through this dialogue several times with her mother and wishing the subject could simply be dropped.

'Yes, but how will it benefit Gaetano when your engagement is broken off again?' Jasmine prompted. 'That's the bit I don't get.'

Poppy didn't really get it either but kept that to herself. How was she supposed to know what went on in Gaetano's multifaceted brain? Apart from anything else she'd had hardly any contact with him since that hotel breakfast they'd shared. He had phoned her with instructions and information about arrangements for her mother and travel plans, but he had not returned to the hall. In the meantime, a new housekeeper had moved into Woodfield Hall and Poppy assumed that the giant refrigerator was being kept fully stocked and vases of flowers were now once again decorating the mansion for the owner who never visited. Gaetano had dismissed Poppy's opinions with an assurance that made it clear that his household arrangements were not and never would be any of her business.

The helicopter picked them up at two in the afternoon. Poppy had packed for both her and her mother, who was being taken to the clinic. Jasmine was nervous and not entirely sober when they boarded and fairly shaky on her legs by the time they landed in London, leaning on her daughter's arm for support.

Gaetano, however, didn't even notice Jasmine Arnold. He was too busy watching Poppy stroll towards him with that lithe, lazy walk of hers. She wore black and red plaid leggings and a black tee, her hair falling in wind-tousled curls round her heart-shaped face. He saw other men taking a second glance at her and it annoyed him. She was unusual and it gave her a distinction that he couldn't quite put a label on but one quality she had in spades and that was sex appeal, he acknowledged grimly, struggling to maintain control of what lay south of his belt. He would get accustomed to her and that response would fade because nothing, not one single intimate thing, was going to take place between them. This was business and he was no soft touch.

The staff member from the clinic designated to pick up Jasmine intercepted Poppy and her mother. The women parted with a hug and tears in their eyes, for the guidelines of Jasmine's treatment plan had warned that the clinic preferred there to be no contact between their patients and families during the first few weeks of treatment. That was why Poppy's first view of Gaetano was blurred because she had been watching her mother nervously walk away and, while knowing that she was doing the best thing possible for her troubled parent, she still felt horribly guilty about it.

'Poppy...' Gaetano murmured, one of his security men taking immediate charge of her luggage trolley.

His lean, darkly handsome features swam through the glimmer of tears in her wide eyes and sliced right through her detachment. He looked utterly gorgeous, sheathed in designer jeans and a casual white and blue striped shirt that accentuated the glow of his bronzed skin colour. For a split second, Poppy simply stared in search of a flaw in his classically beautiful face. At some stage she stopped breathing without realising it and, connecting with dark golden eyes the same shade as melting honey, she suddenly felt so hot she was vaguely surprised that people didn't rush up with fire extinguishers to put out the blaze. Her heartbeat thumped as the noise of their surroundings inexplicably ebbed. A little tweaking sensation in her pelvis caused her to shift her feet while her nipples pinched full and tight below her tee.

'G-Gaetano…' she stammered, barely able to find her voice as she fought a desperate rearguard reaction to what she belatedly realised was a very dangerous susceptibility to Gaetano's magnetic attraction.

Gaetano was taking in the tenting prominence of her nipples below her top and idly wondering what colour they were, arousal moving thickly and hungrily through his blood as he studied her lush pink mouth. 'We're going straight back to my house,' he told her brusquely, snapping back to full attention. 'You've got work to do this evening.'

'Work?' Poppy parroted in surprise as she fell into step by his side.

'I've made up some prompt sheets for you to cover the sort of details you would be expected to know about me if we were in a genuine relationship,' he explained. 'Once you memorise all that we'll be ready to go tomorrow.'

'Tomorrow?' She gasped in dismay because seemingly he wasn't giving her any time at all to practise her new role or even prepare for it.

'It's Rodolfo's seventy-fifth birthday and he's

throwing an afternoon party. Obviously we will be attending it as an engaged couple,' Gaetano explained smoothly.

Nerves clenched and twisted in Poppy's uneasy tummy. She had probably met Rodolfo Leonetti at some stage but she had no memory of the occasion and could only recall seeing him in the distance at the hall when he had still lived there. She had known his late wife, Serafina, well, however, and remembered her clearly. Gaetano's grandmother had been a lovely woman, who treated everyone the same, be they rich or poor, family or staff. Alongside Jasmine, Serafina had taught Poppy how to bake. Recollecting that, Poppy knew exactly what she would be doing in terms of a gift for the older man's birthday.

Her cases were stowed in the sleek expensive car Gaetano had brought to the airport. Damien could probably have told her everything about the vehicle because he was a car buff, but Poppy was too busy marvelling that Gaetano had taken the time to come and pick her up personally and that he was actually driving himself.

His phone rang as they left the airport behind. It was in hands-free mode and the voluble burst of Italian that banished the silence in the car only made Poppy feel more out on a limb than ever. She had to toughen up, she told herself firmly, and regain her confidence. Gaetano had given her the equivalent of a high-paid job and she planned to do the best she could to meet his no doubt high expectations but secretly, deep down inside where only she knew how she felt, Poppy was totally terrified of doing something wrong and letting Gaetano down.

Gaetano was so incredibly particular, she reflected absently, recalling the look on his face when she'd eaten her chocolate cereal with her fingers. Even little mistakes would probably irritate Gaetano. He wasn't tolerant or understanding. No, Poppy knew it wasn't going to be easy to fake anything to Gaetano's satisfaction. In fact she reckoned she was in for a long, hard walk down a road strewn with endless obstacles. While the animated dialogue in Italian went on for what seemed a very long time, Poppy looked out at the busy London streets. Once or twice when she glanced in the other direction she noted the aggressive angle of Gaetano's jaw line that suggested tension and picked up on the hard edge to his dark-timbre drawl and clipped responses.

'Our goose has been cooked,' Gaetano breathed curtly when the phone call was over. 'That was Rodolfo. He wants to meet you now.'

'Now...like right now, *today*?' Poppy exclaimed in dismay.

'Like right now,' Gaetano growled. 'And you're not ready.'

Poppy's eyes flashed. 'And whose fault is that?'

'What do you mean?'

'You shouldn't have waited until the last possible moment to clue me up on what I'm supposed to know about you,' Poppy pointed out without hesitation. 'Sensible people prepare for anything important *more* than one day in advance.'

'Don't you dare start criticising me!' Gaetano erupted, sharply disconcerting her as he flashed a look of angry, flaming censure. 'It's more than twenty-four hours since I even slept. We've had a crisis deal at the bank and this stupid business was the very last thing on my mind.'

'If it's so stupid you can forget about it again.' Poppy proffered that get-out clause stiffly. 'Don't mind me. This was, after all, *your* idea, *all* your idea.'

'I can't forget about it again when I've already told Rodolfo I'm engaged!' Gaetano launched back at her furiously. 'Whether I like it or not, I'm *stuck* with you and faking it!'

'Oh, goody…aren't I the lucky girl?' Poppy murmured in a poisonous undertone intended to sting. 'You're such a catch, Gaetano. All that money and success but not a single ounce of charm!'

'Be quiet!' Gaetano raked at her with incredulity.

'Go stuff yourself!' Poppy tossed back fierily as he shot the car to a halt outside a tall town house in a fancy street embellished with a central garden.

'And you're stuck with me,' Gaetano asserted with grim satisfaction as he closed her wrist in a grip of steel to prevent her leaping out of the car. He flipped open the ring box in his other hand and removed the diamond engagement ring to shove it onto her wedding finger with no ceremony whatsoever.

'Oh, dear...ugly ring alert,' Poppy snapped, studying the huge diamond solitaire with unappreciative eyes. 'Of course, it's one of those fake diamonds...right?'

'Of course it's not a fake!' Gaetano bit out, what little patience he had decimated by lack of sleep and her unexpectedly challenging behaviour.

'It's hard to believe that you can spend that much money and end up with something that looks like it fell out of a Christmas cracker.' Poppy groaned. 'I can't go in there, Gaetano.'

'Get out of the car,' he urged, leaning across to

open the door for her. 'Of course you can go in there and wing it. Just look all intoxicated with your ring.'

'Yes, getting drunk in receipt of this non-example of good taste would certainly be under-standable.'

'You're supposed to be in love with me!' Gaetano roared at her.

'Trouble is, you're about as loveable as a grizzly bear,' Poppy opined, walking round the bonnet and up onto the pavement. 'My acting skills may be poor but yours are a great deal worse.'

'What the hell are you talking about?' Gaetano squared up to her, six feet four inches of roaring aggression and impatience. 'It's time to stop messing about and start acting.'

Poppy lifted a hand and stabbed his broad muscular chest with a combative forefinger. 'But you *said* you wanted me to be myself. What exactly do you want, Gaetano?'

'*Porca miseria!* I want you to stop driving me insane!' Gaetano bit out wrathfully, backing her up against the wing of the car, long powerful thighs entrapping her. 'I will tell you only once. If you can't do as you're told you're out of here!'

'I'm only just resisting the urge to use some very rude words,' Poppy warned him, standing her ground with defiant green eyes. 'This is all *your* fault. You've dragged me here straight from the airport knowing I'm not remotely prepared for this meeting.'

And for Gaetano, whose aggressive need to dominate had emerged in the nursery when he had systematically bullied his first nanny into letting him do pretty much whatever he wanted, that resistance was like a red rag to a bull. Totally unaware of anything beyond the overwhelming desire to touch her while forcing her to do what he wanted her to do, Gaetano snapped an arm round her and kissed her.

His mouth slammed down on hers and it was as if the world stopped dead and then closed round that moment. She was in such a rage with him, it was a reflex reaction for Poppy to close her teeth together, refusing him entry. He shifted against her, all lean, sinuous, powerful male, and the erection she could feel nudging against her stomach sent the most overwhelming awareness shimmying through her like a dangerous drug. The heat and strength of him against her was even more arousing and she unclamped her teeth for him, helpless in the grip of the driving hunger that had captured her and destroyed her opposition.

With a hungry groan, his tongue eased into her mouth and it was without a doubt the most heart-stopping instant of sensation she had ever experienced as his tongue teased and tangled with hers before plunging deep. An ache she had never felt in a man's arms before hollowed almost painfully at the heart of her and she was pushing instinctively against him even as he urged her back against the car, so that they were welded together so tight a card couldn't have slid between them. Her arms went round him, massaging up over his wide shoulders before sliding up to lace into his luxuriant black hair and then raking down again over his muscled arms to spread across his taut masculine ass. It was a mindless, addictive, totally visceral embrace.

In an abrupt movement, Gaetano stepped back from her, his breathing audible, sawing in and out of his big chest as if he had run a marathon. Poppy was all over the place mentally and she blinked, literally struggling to return to the real world while fighting a shocking desire to yank him bodily back to her. He was so hot at kissing she was ready to spontaneously combust. He might not have an ounce of charm but when it came to the sex stuff he was out at the front of the field, she decided, a burning blush warming her face as she too worked to get her breath back.

'Well…that was interesting,' she remarked shakily, feeling the need to say something, anything that might suggest that she had regained control when she had not.

Gaetano, who never, *ever* did PDAs with women, was horribly aware of his bodyguards standing by staring as if a little Martian had taken his place. In short, Gaetano was in shock but he also knew that if he had been parked somewhere private he would have had Poppy spread across the bonnet while he plunged into her lithe body hard and fast and sated the appalling level of hunger coursing through his lower body. He ached; he ached so bad he wanted to groan out loud. Dark colour etched the line of his high cheekbones.

'Let's go inside,' he suggested in a driven undertone. 'Just take your lead from me, *bella mia*.'

And won't doing exactly as Gaetano tells you be fun? a little devil enquired inside Poppy's bemused head. If it had related to kissing, she would have been queuing up, she conceded numbly. Nobody had ever made her feel so much with one kiss. In fact she hadn't known it was even possible to be that turned on by a man after just one kiss. Gaetano had hidden depths, dark, sexy depths, but she had not the smallest intention of plumbing those depths…

CHAPTER FOUR

'I SAW YOU ARRIVE,' Rodolfo Leonetti volunteered, disconcerting his grandson. 'It looked as though you were having words.'

Poppy almost froze by Gaetano's side, her discomfiture sweeping through her like a tidal wave. Gaetano's grandfather didn't look his age. With his head of wavy grey hair and the upright stature of a much younger man, not to mention a height not far short of Gaetano's, he still looked strong and vital. He greeted her with a kiss on both cheeks and smiled warmly at her before unleashing that unsettling comment on Gaetano.

'We were having a row,' Poppy was taken aback to hear Gaetano admit. 'Poppy doesn't like her engagement ring. Perhaps I should have taken her with me to choose it…'

Rodolfo widened his shrewd dark eyes. 'My grandson left you out of that selection?'

Pink and flustered by the speed with which Gaetano plotted and reacted in a tight corner, Poppy said, 'I'm afraid so...' In an uncertain movement she extended her hand for the older man to study the ring.

'You could see that diamond from outer space,' Rodolfo remarked, straight-faced.

'It's beautiful,' Poppy hastened to add.

'Be honest, you hate it,' Gaetano encouraged, having told the story, clearly happy to go with the flow.

'It's too bling for me,' she murmured dutifully, sinking down into the comfortable seat Rodolfo had indicated. Her nerves were strung so tight that her very face felt stiff with tension. She barely had the awareness to take in the beautiful big reception room, which strongly resembled the splendour of the reception rooms at Woodfield Hall.

'I was very sorry to hear about your mother's

problems,' Gaetano's grandfather said while Poppy was pouring the tea, having been invited to do the hostess thing for the first time in her life. She almost dropped the teapot at Rodolfo's quietly offered expression of sympathy. Evidently Gaetano had been honest about her mother's predicament. 'I'm sure the clinic will help her.'

'I hope so.' Poppy compressed her lips as Rodolfo got to his feet and excused himself. As the door swung in his wake, Poppy groaned out loud. 'I'm no good at this, Gaetano—'

'You'll improve. He must've seen us kissing. That will have at least made us look like a proper couple,' he pointed out soft and low. 'Sometimes not having a script is better.'

'I would work better from a script.' She slanted a glance at him, encountering smouldering dark golden eyes, and pink surged into her cheeks.

Rodolfo reappeared and sank back into his seat. He had a small box in his hand, which he opened. 'This was your grandmother's ring. As all her jewellery will go to your wife I thought it would be a good idea to let Poppy have a look at Serafina's engagement ring now.'

Poppy stared in astonished recognition at the fine diamond and ruby cluster on display. 'I remember your wife taking it off when she was baking,' she shared quietly. 'It's a fabulous ring.'

'It belongs to you now,' Rodolfo said with gentle courtesy and the sadness in his creased eyes made her eyes sting.

'She was a lovely person,' Poppy whispered shakily.

Gaetano couldn't credit what he was seeing. His fake fiancée and Rodolfo were having a mutual love-in, full of exchanged glances and sentimental smiles of understanding. His grandfather was sliding his beloved late wife's ring onto Poppy's finger as if she were Cinderella having the glass slipper fitted.

'I believe she would have been happy for you to wear it,' the old man said fondly, admiring it on Poppy's hand, the giant diamond solitaire purchased by Gaetano now abandoned on the coffee table.

'Thank you very much,' Poppy responded chokily. 'It's gorgeous.'

'And it comes with a very happy history in its back story,' Rodolfo shared mistily.

Gaetano wanted to groan out loud. He wanted his grandfather to disapprove of Poppy, not welcome her with open arms and start patting her hand while he talked happily about his late wife, Serafina. Of course, a little initial enthusiasm was to be expected, he reasoned shrewdly, and Rodolfo would hardly feel critical in the first fine flush of his approval of the step that Gaetano had taken.

Afternoon tea stretched into dinner, by which time Gaetano was heartily bored with family stories. With admirable tact and patience, however, Poppy had listened with convincing interest to his grandfather recount Leonetti family history. She had much better manners than Gaetano had expected and her easy relaxation with the older man was even more noteworthy because few people relaxed around Rodolfo, who was considerably more clever and ruthless than he appeared. If Poppy had been his real fiancée, Gaetano would have been ecstatic at the warmth of her reception. Indeed one could have been forgiven for thinking that Rodolfo had waited his entire life praying for the joy of seeing his grandson bring the housekeeper's daughter home and announce that he was planning to marry her. Only when Poppy began smothering yawns did Gaetano's torture end.

'Time for us to leave.' Gaetano tugged a drooping Poppy out of her seat with a powerful hand.

'Hope we don't have to go far,' she mumbled sleepily.

Encountering the older man's startled glance at his bride-to-be's ignorance, Gaetano straightened and smiled. 'She hasn't been here before,' he pointed out. 'I wanted to surprise her.'

'What surprise?' Poppy pressed as he walked her out of the drawing room.

'Rodolfo had an entire wing of this house converted for me to occupy ten years ago,' he told her, throwing wide a door at the foot of the corridor. 'All we have to do is walk through a connecting door and we're in my space.'

And even drowsy as she was it was very obvious to Poppy that Gaetano's part of the house was a hugely different space. Rich colours, heavy fabrics and polished antiques were replaced by contemporary stone floors, pale colours and plain furniture. It was as distinct as night was to day from his grandfather's house. 'Elegant,' she commented.

'I'm glad you think so.' Gaetano showed her upstairs into the master bedroom. 'This is where we sleep...'

Poppy froze, her brain snapping into gear again. *'We?'*

'We can't stay this close to Rodolfo and pretend to be engaged *without* sharing a room,' Gaetano fired back at her impatiently. 'His staff service this place as well as his.'

'But you didn't *warn* me about this!' Poppy objected. 'Naturally I assumed you had an apartment somewhere on your own where I'd have my own room.'

'Well, you can't have your own room here,' Gaetano informed her without apology. 'Doubtless Rodolfo would like to think you're the vestal-virgin type, but he wouldn't find it credible that I had asked you to marry me...'

Poppy studied the huge divan sleigh bed and her soft mouth compressed. 'For goodness' sake, there's only one bed...and I'm not sharing it with you!'

'You have to sleep in here with me. There's a downside for both of us in this arrangement,' Gaetano countered grimly.

'And what's *your* downside?' Poppy asked with interest.

'Celibacy,' Gaetano intoned very drily. 'I can't risk being seen or associated with any other woman while I'm supposed to be engaged to you.'

'Oh, dear...' Poppy commented without an

atom of sympathy. 'From what I've read about your usual pursuits in the press, that will be a character-building challenge for you.'

Exasperation laced Gaetano's lean, darkly handsome features. He would never ever hurt a woman but there were times when he wanted to plunge Poppy head first into a mud bath. 'There's a lot of rubbish talked about my private life in the newspapers.'

'That line might work with one of your social-ites, Gaetano…but *not* with me. I know that party *did* take place and what happened at it.'

Gaetano fought the urge to defend himself and collided with her witchy green eyes and momen-tarily forgot what he had been about to say. 'I'm going for a shower,' he said instead and began to undress.

Leonetti flesh alert! screamed a little voice in Poppy's head as Gaetano shed his shirt without inhibition. And why would he be inhibited when he was unveiling a work of art? He was all sleek muscle from the vee above his lean hips to the corrugated muscular flatness of his abdomen and the swelling power of his pectoral muscles. Her mouth ran dry. She might not be the vestal-virgin type but she *was* a virgin and she had never shared a room with a half-naked male before. That was not information she planned to share with Gaetano, especially as she pretty much blamed him for the reality that she had yet to take that sexual plunge in adulthood.

At sixteen, after his rejection, she had almost decided to have sex with someone else but had realised what she was doing in time and had called a halt before things got out of hand. She wasn't proud of that episode, well aware that she had acted like a bit of a tease with the boy concerned. Her real lesson had been grasping that going off to have mindless sex with someone else because Gaetano didn't want her was pathetic and silly. While she was at college doing her nursing training she had had boyfriends and occasional little moments of temptation but nobody had tempted her as much as Gaetano had once tempted her.

And Poppy was stubborn and had decided that she would only sleep with someone when she really, *really* wanted to. She wasn't going to have sex just because some man expected it of her, nor was she planning to have sex just for the sake of it.

Poppy opened one of her cases and only then appreciated that her luggage had already been unpacked for her. So this was how the rich lived, she thought ruefully, wondering what she was going to use as pyjamas when she didn't ever wear them because she preferred to sleep naked. She had nothing big enough to cover her decently in mixed company and she rifled through Gaetano's drawers to borrow a big white tee shirt that was both large and sexless. He might have forgotten that kiss, that terrifying surge of limitless hunger...but she hadn't and she had no plans to tempt fate.

Gaetano was thinking about sex in the shower and wondering if Poppy would consider broadening their agreement. He wanted her and she wanted him. To his outlook that was a simple balanced equation and it made sense that they should make the most of each other for the duration of their relationship. It was the practical solution and Gaetano was always practical, particularly when it came to his high sex drive.

A towel knotted round his lean hips, Gaetano trod back into the bedroom. Poppy took one look at all that bronzed skin still sprinkled with drops of water and realised that she wanted to lick him like a postage stamp. With a stifled groan at her own atrocious weakness, she pushed past him and went into the bathroom to get changed.

Gaetano pulled on boxers on the grounds that it never paid to take anything for granted with women and that doing so only annoyed them. Poppy emerged from the bathroom wearing what could only be one of his tee shirts because it hung off her slender frame in loose folds. Even so, it still couldn't hide the prominent little peaks of her breasts, the womanly curve of her hips or the perfection of the long shapely legs below the hem.

'I have a suggestion to make,' Gaetano murmured huskily.

'Do I want to hear this?' Poppy wisecracked, pushing back the bedding and scrambling into the bed, feeling her limbs settle into an incredibly soft and supportive mattress that was a far cry from the ancient lumpy bed of her youth. Wearing only silk boxers Gaetano was an outrageously masculine presence and very hard for Poppy to ignore. She was trying to respect his space by not looking at him and hoping he would award her the same courtesy of acting as though she were still fully clothed.

'We have to pretend to be lovers,' Gaetano pointed out.

Wondering in what possible direction that statement could be travelling, Poppy prompted, 'Yes…so?'

'Why don't we make it real?' Gaetano drawled, smooth as melted honey.

Her vocal cords went into arrest and respecting his space suddenly became much too challenging. *'Real?'* Poppy exclaimed loudly. 'What exactly do you mean by real?'

'You're not that innocent,' Gaetano assured her lazily as he sprang into bed beside her.

'So, you're suggesting that we have sex because you don't fancy celibacy?' Poppy enquired, delicate auburn brows raised in disbelief.

'We are stuck in this situation,' Gaetano reminded her.

'I can live without sex,' Poppy told him tightly, feeling colour climb hotly towards her hairline because even saying 'sex' in Gaetano's presence made her feel horribly self-conscious.

'I can as well but not happily,' Gaetano told her bluntly. 'We're very attracted to each other. We might as well make the most of it.'

'Any port in a storm?' Poppy remarked without amusement. 'I'm here in the bed and, as you see it, available, so I should be interested?'

Gaetano leant closer, his stubbled jaw line

propped on the heel of his upraised hand as he gazed down at her with absolutely gorgeous dark golden eyes. 'I'm good, *bella mia*. You wouldn't be disappointed.'

Poppy was as frozen with fear as a woman facing a hungry cannibal might be. But insidious heat and dampness were welling in the tender place between her thighs, striving to work their wicked seductive magic on her resistance. In fact she could feel her whole body literally wake up, sit up and take notice of Gaetano's offer. He was offering her what she had once desperately wanted but on terms she could never accept. 'I don't want to be used.'

'I'm surprised you're so narrow in your outlook. Wouldn't you be using me to scratch the same itch?' Gaetano enquired softly.

Her whole face flamed and she flipped over on her side, turning her narrow back defensively on him. Get thee behind me, Satan, she thought helplessly. 'No, thanks,' she said chokily, unsure whether she wanted to laugh or cry at his blunt proposition. 'If I want meaningless sex I imagine I can get it just about anywhere.'

Gaetano stroked a long brown forefinger down her taut spinal cord. 'Sex with me wouldn't be meaningless. It would be amazing. You set me on fire, *gioia mia*.'

Poppy rolled her eyes. He was so slick and full of confidence but that caressing touch lingered with her, lighting up little pockets of melting willingness inside her treacherous body. 'I'll keep it in mind. If my itch has to be scratched I will seriously consider you,' she lied stonily.

'What more do you want from me?' Gaetano asked silkily. 'I'm honest. I'm clean. I don't lie or cheat.'

'It doesn't stop you from being a four-letter word of a man,' Poppy told him roundly. 'I thought Italian lovers were supposed to be the last word in seduction. You just turned me off big time.'

'I was respecting your intelligence by not shooting you a line,' Gaetano traded with husky amusement that laced through his dark deep drawl in a sexy, accented purr.

Poppy pictured herself flipping over and slapping him so hard his perfect teeth rattled in his too ingenious head. Her own teeth gritted aggressively. Without warning she was also imagining easing back into the hard, allmale heat of him while his arms closed round her and his hips moved against hers. And that sensual imagery was so energising that she felt boiling hot all over. Her nipples swelled and prickled and the heat in her pelvis mushroomed. Her face burned with shame in the darkness. Wanting was wanting, she reasoned with the sexual side of her nature, but it wasn't enough on its own. Gaetano wasn't the man for her, she reminded herself doggedly.

'You know, if you were a nice guy—'

'When did I ever say I was a nice guy?' Gaetano cut in sharply.

'You didn't,' Poppy conceded grudgingly, turning over to pick out the powerful silhouette of his head and shoulders in the dim light. 'But you shouldn't be thinking about your sex life. Right now you should be worrying more about how your grandfather is going to feel when this engagement falls through. Because he's making such an effort to be welcoming and accepting of someone like me, I think he'll be devastated when our relationship comes to nothing.'

'Allow me to know my own grandfather better than you.'

'You're too focused on your career plan to see beyond it. What I saw today was that Rodolfo was incredibly happy about you getting engaged. How could he be anything other than upset when it breaks down?'

Gaetano grimaced and flung his dark head back against the pillows. She didn't understand. How could she? He could hardly tell her that she was supposed to bomb as a fiancée so that her disappearance from his life again would be more worthy of celebration than disappointment. Time would take care of that problem. After all, she had most likely been on her very best behaviour at her first meeting with his grandfather and sooner rather than later she would probably let herself down.

'You used to swear a lot,' he remarked out of the blue.

'I picked it up at school because everyone used bad language. For a while I did it deliberately because I was being bullied and I was desperate to fit in,' she confided.

'Did it make a difference?'

'No,' she admitted with a wry laugh. 'Nothing I wore or did or said could make me cool. Being plump with red hair and living at Woodfield Hall with "those posh bastards" was a supreme provocation to the other pupils.'

'What did the bullies do?'

Thinking of her getting bullied, Gaetano was experiencing an extraordinary desire to pull her into his arms and comfort her. But he didn't do comforting. Indeed he was downright unnerved by that perverse impulse and he actually shifted as far away from her as he could get and still be in the same bed.

'All the usual. Name calling, tripping me up, nasty rumours and messages and texts,' she recited wearily. 'I hated school, couldn't wait to get out of there. Once I was out, I stopped swearing as soon as I realised it offended people.'

He was tempted to tell her that she had never been plump. She had simply developed her womanly curves before she shot up in height. But right then he didn't want to talk and he didn't want to think about curves, womanly or otherwise. His hunger for her was making him uncomfortable and that infuriated him because Gaetano had never hungered that much for one particular woman. Beautiful women had always been pretty much interchangeable for him. It was the challenge, he told himself impatiently. He only wanted her because she was saying no. But that simplistic belief didn't ease his tension in the slightest. It was, he decided grimly, likely to feel like a *very* long engagement.

* * *

First thing in the morning, Poppy looked amazing, Gaetano conceded hours later, studying her from across the bedroom. Her red hair streamed like a banner across the pale bedding, framing her delicate face and the rosebud pout of her lips. A narrow shoulder protruded from below his slipped tee shirt and the sheet was pushed back to bare one leg from knee to slender ankle. And that easily, that quickly, Gaetano had a hard-on again and gritted his teeth in annoyance. What the hell was it about her? He felt like a man trying to fight an invisible illness!

'Poppy…?'

She shifted in the bed, lashes fluttering up on luminous green eyes. 'Gaetano…?' she whispered drowsily.

'I left that prompt sheet I meant you to study last night on the desk in my home office. I'll see you at Rodolfo's party at three.'

Poppy sat up in a panic. 'What will I wear?'

'Your usual clothes. Be yourself,' he reminded her as he vanished out of the door.

Poppy scrambled out of bed to follow him. 'Where are you going?'

Gaetano swung round and sent her a pained appraisal. 'Work…the bank.'

'Oh…' Having asked what appeared to be a stupid question, Poppy ducked hastily back into the bedroom and went for a shower while planning her own day.

First of all she had to go and buy the ingredients for her present for Rodolfo's seventy-fifth. She could only hope that she wasn't getting it wrong in the gift department. After that she had a rather more pressing need to attend to: finding work for herself. She had just about enough money in her purse to make Rodolfo's cake but she had nothing more and no savings to fall back on.

The sleek granite-topped kitchen had a fridge packed with food and a very large selection of chocolate cereals that made her smile. Gaetano had remembered her preference. She ate while she studied the prompt sheets he had mentioned. It was like a CV written for a job: qualifications listed, sports pursuits outlined, not a single reference to any memorable moments. He just had no idea of the sort of things that a woman in love would want to know about him, Poppy reflected ruefully. When was his birthday? What was his favourite colour?

She texted him to ask.

Gaetano suppressed a groan when his phone buzzed yet again and lifted it to see what the latest irrelevant question was.

Who was the first woman you fell in love with?

He had never been in love and he was proud of it.

What do you value most in a woman?

Independence, he texted back.

As Poppy walked round the supermarket with her shopping list she raised her brows. If he liked independent women why did he always date clingy airheads? So, she asked that too and they began to argue by text until she was laughing. Gaetano had an image of himself that did not always match reality. She could have told him that he dated clingy airheads because they did as they were told, accepted his workaholic schedule and made few demands.

Noticing a 'help wanted' sign in the window of a café she called in, enjoyed an interview on the spot and was hired to work a shift that very evening. Relieved to have solved the problem of being broke, she returned to the town house by the separate entrance at the side and proceeded to mess up Gaetano's basically unused kitchen with her baking session. She settled the cake into the cake carrier she had bought for the purpose and set the birthday card on top of it before going to get changed.

She wore a tartan skirt with black lace stockings and high heels. Gaetano wolf-whistled the instant he saw her. 'Wow...' he breathed with quiet masculine appreciation. 'Your legs are to die for...'

'Really?' Poppy grinned and then frowned doubtfully. 'Is this phase one of the Italian seduction routine?'

'You're very suspicious.'

'I don't trust you,' Poppy told him truthfully. 'I think being sneaky would come naturally to you.'

'I've never had to be sneaky with women,' Gaetano told her truthfully.

The drawing room was crowded with guests when they arrived. The instant Poppy saw the fancy cocktail-type frocks and delicate jewellery that the other women sported and the stares that her informal outfit attracted, she paled in dismay. She stuck out like a sore thumb and hated the feeling, squirming discomfiture taking her by storm and reminding her of her days at school when no matter how hard she'd tried she had always failed to fit in. Remembering that Gaetano had urged her to be herself was not a consolation because her unconventional appearance *had* to be an embarrassment to him. How could it be anything else?

Gaetano's grandfather made a major production out of welcoming them and announcing their engagement. Poppy's guilt over their deception sent colour flying into her cheeks but she saw only satisfaction in Gaetano's brilliant smile and from it she deduced that everything was going the way he had planned.

But Poppy was wrong in that assumption. She served Rodolfo with the strawberry layer cake with mascarpone-cheese icing that was his favourite and which she had learned to bake at his wife's side. His eyes went all watery and he gave her an almost boyish grin as he took up the cake knife she passed him and cut himself a large helping.

'So, when's the big day?' he asked Poppy within Gaetano's hearing.

Gaetano tensed. 'We haven't set a date as yet...'

'You don't want to risk a treasure like Poppy

getting away,' his grandfather warned him softly, shrewd eyes resting on his grandson's lean, darkly handsome face. 'I don't believe in long engagements.'

'We don't want to rush in either,' Poppy remarked carefully, instinct sending her to Gaetano's rescue.

'Next month would be a good time for me before I head off to Italy for the summer,' Rodolfo pointed out calmly.

'We'll talk it over,' Gaetano fielded smoothly.

'And when you get back from your honeymoon,' the old man delivered cheerfully, 'it will be as CEO.'

Gaetano nodded, thoroughly disconcerted and fighting not to betray the fact that he knew that his promotion was now a *marriage* step away from him. He studied Poppy from below his black lashes. Against all the odds, Rodolfo adored her. Trust Poppy to bake his grandmother's signature cake. She couldn't have done anything more likely to please and impress. She had ticked his grandfather's every box. Not only was she beautiful, kind and thoughtful, she could actually *cook*. Gaetano experienced a hideous 'hoist with his own petard' sensation and wondered how the hell he was going to climb back out of the hole he had dug.

CHAPTER FIVE

'WHY ARE YOU in such a hurry?' Gaetano frowned as Poppy sped away from him towards the bedroom. His grandfather had outmanoeuvred him and he needed to have a serious conversation with his fake fiancée.

'I have to get changed and get out in the next... er...ten minutes!' she exclaimed in dismay, hastening her step after checking her watch.

Gaetano took his time about strolling down to the bedroom where Poppy was engaged in pulling on a pair of jeans, lithe long legs topped by a pair of bright red knickers on display. Her face flushing, she half turned away, wriggling her shapely hips to ease up the jeans. The enthusiastic stirring at his groin was uniquely unwelcome to Gaetano at that moment. 'Where do you have to be in ten minutes?' he asked quietly.

'Work. I picked up a waitressing shift at the café round the corner. I'll be back by midnight,' she told him chirpily.

In the doorway, Gaetano went rigid, convinced that he could not have heard her correctly. 'You applied for a job as a *waitress*...' his dark deep drawl climbed tellingly in volume and emphasis as he spoke that word '...while you're pretending to be engaged to me?'

'Why not? Bartending is better paid but the café was closer and the hours are casual and flexible and that would probably suit you better.'

Brilliant dark eyes landed on her with the chilling effect of an ice bath. 'You working as a waitress doesn't suit me in *any* way.'

'I don't see why you should object,' Poppy reasoned, thrusting her feet into her comfy ankle boots. 'I mean, you're still working and what am I supposed to do with myself while you're busy all day? It's not even as if pretending to be your fiancée is a full-time job.'

'As far as I'm concerned, it *is* full-time and you will go to the café now and tell them that you're sorry but you won't be working there to-night,' Gaetano told her with raking impatience. '*Diavelos!* Do I have to spell every little thing out to you? I'm a billionaire banker. You can't work in a café or a bar for peanuts while you're purportedly engaged to me!'

An angry flush had lit up Poppy's cheeks. 'Then what am I supposed to do for money?'

'If you need money, I'll give it to you,' Gaetano declared, pulling out his wallet, relieved that the problem could be so easily fixed. But seriously, where was her brain? Working as a waitress while living in a mansion?

Poppy backed away a step and then snaked past him in the doorway to trudge down to the hall. 'I don't want your money, Gaetano. I *work* for my money. I don't take handouts from anyone.'

'But I'm the exception to that rule,' Gaetano

slotted in grimly as he followed her with tenacious resolve. 'While you are engaged to me, you are not allowed to embarrass me by working in a low-paid menial job.'

Outraged by that decree, Poppy whirled round to face him again, the hank of hair from her ponytail falling over her shoulder in a bright colourful stream. 'Is that a fact?' she prompted. 'Well, I'm sorry, you're out of luck on this one. As far as I'm concerned, any kind of honest work is preferable to living off charity and I don't care if you think waitressing is menial—'

'We have a deal!' Gaetano raked at her with raw bite. 'You're breaking it!'

'At no stage did you ever mention that I would not be able to take paid work,' Poppy flung back at him in furious denial. 'So, don't try to deviously change the rules to suit yourself. I'm sorry if you see me working as a waitress at Carrie's coffee shop as a major embarrassment. Don't you have enough status on your own account? Does it really matter what I do? I would remind you that I am an ordinary girl who needs to work to live and that's not about to change for you or anyone else!'

'It's totally unnecessary for you to work…in fact it's *preposterous*!' Gaetano slammed back at her loudly, dark eyes flaring as golden as the heart of a fire now, his anger unconcealed. 'Particularly when I have already assured you that I will cover your every expense while you are staying in London.'

'Just as I've already told you,' Poppy proclaimed heatedly, 'I will *not* accept money from you. I'm an independent woman and I have my pride. If our positions were reversed, would you want me keeping you?'

'Don't be ridiculous!' Gaetano roared back, all control of his temper abandoned in the face of her continuing refusal to listen to him and respect his opinion. Never before in his life had a woman opposed him in such a way.

More intimidated than she was prepared to admit or show by the depth of his anger and the sheer size of him towering over her while he gave forth as if he were voicing the Ten Commandments, Poppy brought up her chin. 'I'm not being ridiculous,' she countered obstinately. 'I'm standing up for what I believe in. I don't want your money. I want my own. And as only a few people know I'm engaged to you, I don't see how it's going to embarrass you. Especially as you don't embarrass that easily.'

'And what's that supposed to mean?' he demanded.

Poppy dealt him an accusing look. 'You should've given me some pointers on what to wear at the birthday party. Once I saw how the other women were dressed, I felt stupid.'

Gaetano shrugged. 'It wasn't important. I want you to be yourself,' he repeated dismissively. 'As for the waitress job—'

'I'm keeping it!' Poppy incised, lifting her chin combatively because she was needled by his assurance that being the odd one out in the fashion stakes at the party was something she should simply be able to shrug off. Had that been a rap on the knuckles? Was she oversensitive? Too prone to feeling inadequate?

'And that's your last word on the subject?' Gaetano growled as she yanked open the front side door, which serviced his wing of the house.

'I'm afraid so,' Poppy declared before she raced off at speed, pulling the door shut behind her.

'If you don't watch out, you'll lose her,' a voice said from behind Gaetano.

In consternation, he swung round to focus on his grandfather, who was wedged in the doorway communicating between the two properties. 'How much of that did you hear?' Gaetano asked tautly.

'With this door open I couldn't help overhearing the last part of your argument,' Rodolfo Leonetti advanced. 'I'll admit to hearing enough to appreciate that my grandson is a hopeless snob. She was correct, Gaetano. There can never be shame in honest work. Your grandmother insisted on selling her father's fish at a stall until the day she married me.'

'Your wife was raised on a tiny backward island in a different era. Times have changed,' Gaetano parried thinly.

Rodolfo laughed with sincere appreciation. 'Women don't change that much. Poppy's not interested in your money. Do you realise how very lucky you are to have found such a woman?'

In silence, Gaetano jerked his aggressive chin in acknowledgement. He was still climbing back down from the dizzy heights of the unholy rage Poppy's defiance had lit inside him, marvelling at how angry she had made him while being disconcerted by his loss of control. His lean hands flexed into fists before slowly loosening again.

'And as her temper seems to be as hot as your own it may well take some very nifty moves on your part to keep her,' his grandfather opined with quiet assurance as he strolled back through the communicating door.

Gaetano struck the wall with a knotted fist and

swore long and low beneath his breath. Poppy set his temper off like a rocket, not a problem he had ever had with a woman before. That's because you date 'clingy airheads', a voice chimed in the back of his mind, an exact quote of Poppy's text that sounded remarkably like her. He gritted his teeth, tension pulling like tight strings in his lean, powerful body to tauten every muscle group. It was stress caused by the lack of sex, he decided abruptly. A wave of relief for that rational explanation for his recent irrational behaviour engulfed him. Gaetano didn't like anything that he couldn't understand. Yet Poppy fell into that category and he knew he didn't dislike her.

Poppy worked her shift in the café, her mind buzzing like a busy bee throughout. Had she been too hard on Gaetano? It was true that he was a snob but what else could he be after the over-privileged life he had led since birth? But Rodolfo's clear desire to rush his grandson into marriage had shocked Gaetano and naturally that had put him in a bad mood, she conceded ruefully. Evidently when Gaetano had suggested their fake engagement he had seriously underestimated the extent of his grandfather's enthusiasm for marrying him off. Only an actual wedding was going to satisfy Rodolfo Leonetti and move Gaetano up the last crucial step of his career ladder. An engagement wasn't going to achieve that for him, which pretty much meant that everything Gaetano had so far done had been for nothing.

When Poppy finished work, she was astonished to glance out of the window and see Gaetano waiting outside for her. Street light fell on his defined cheekbones, strong nose and stubbled jaw line. One glance at his undeniable hotness and he took her breath away. Why had he come to meet her? Colour washing her face, she pulled her coat out of the back room and waited for the manager to unlock the door for her exit. Gaetano's gaze, dark, deep-set and pure gold, flamed and he moved forward.

'What are you doing here?' she asked to fill the tense silence.

'You can't walk back to the house on your own at this time of night,' Gaetano told her.

'Well, I suppose you would think that way,' Poppy remarked, inclining her head to acknowledge his bodyguards ranged across the pavement mere yards from them. Gaetano was never ever alone in the way that other ordinary people were alone. 'Why didn't you just send one of them to look out for me?'

'I owed you,' Gaetano breathed, unlocking the sleek sports car by the kerb. 'I was out of line earlier.'

'You get out of line a lot...but that's the first time you've admitted it,' Poppy said uncertainly.

Gaetano swung in beside her and in the confined space she stared at him, her breath hitching in her throat, heartbeat thumping very loudly in her eardrums. Black-lashed eyes assailed hers and she fell still, her mouth running dry. He lifted a hand, framed her face with spread fingers and kissed her. Her hand braced on a strong masculine thigh as she leant closer, helplessly hungry for that connection and the heat and pressure of his strong sensual mouth on hers. Her body went haywire, all liquid heat and response as his tongue delved and tangled with hers, and a deep quiver thrummed through her slender length. The wanting gripping her was all powerful, racing through her to swell her breasts and ignite a feverish damp heat between her thighs. In a harried movement, Poppy yanked her head back and forced her trembling body back into the passenger seat. 'What was that for?' she asked shakily.

'I have no excuse or reason. I can't stop wanting to touch you.'

'It wasn't supposed to be like this…with us,' she mumbled accusingly through her swollen lips.

Long brown fingers circled over the top of her knee and roved lazily higher, skating up her inner thigh. 'Tell me, no,' Gaetano urged in a harsh undertone.

'No,' she framed without conviction, legs involuntarily parting because with every fibre of her being she craved his touch.

'You're pushing me off the edge of sanity,' Gaetano growled, shifting position to claim her mouth again. With little passionate nips and licks and bites he took her mouth in a way it had never been taken and sent hot rivers of excitement rolling into her pelvis.

Long fingers stroked over the taut triangle of fabric stretched tight between her thighs, lingering to circle over her core. A warm tingling sensation of almost unbearable excitement gripped her and she bucked beneath his hand, helplessly, wantonly inviting more. Give me more, her body was screaming, shameless in the grip of that need. The fabric that separated her most sensitive flesh from him was a torment but he made no attempt to remove or circumvent its presence. She ground her hips down on the seat, nipples straining and stiff and prickling, the hunger like a voracious animal clawing for more inside her.

That hunger was so terrifyingly strong and her brain felt so befogged with it she shivered, suddenly cold and scared of being overwhelmed.

'This is not cool,' Gaetano whispered against her lips. 'We're in a car in a public street. This is not cool at all, *bella mia*.'

'It's just lust,' she tried to say lightly, dismissively, and she tried to summon a laugh but found she couldn't because there was nothing funny about the power of the physical urges engulfing her or the nasty draining aftermath of blocking and denying those urges.

'Lust has never made me behave like a randy teenager before,' Gaetano growled. 'Around you I have a constant hard-on.'

'Stop it…*stop* talking about it!' Poppy snapped, ramming her trembling hands into the pockets of her flying jacket.

'That's impossible when it's all I can think about.' With a stifled curse he fired the engine of the car. 'But we have more important things to discuss.'

'Yes. Rodolfo called your bluff,' she breathed heavily, struggling to return to the real world again.

'That's not how I would describe what he did. I've been mulling it over all evening,' Gaetano admitted grittily. 'I'm afraid you hit the target last night when you accused me of ignoring the human dimension. I'm great with figures and strategy, not so good with people. But this afternoon looking at Rodolfo and listening to him talk I saw a man aware of his years and afraid he wouldn't live long enough to see the next generation. All my adult life I've read him wrong. I thought all I had to do to please him was to become a success and be everything my father wasn't but it wasn't enough.'

'How wasn't it enough?'

'Rodolfo would have been a much happier man if I'd married straight out of university and given him grandchildren,' Gaetano breathed wryly.

'Why regret what you can't change? Obviously you didn't meet anyone you wanted to marry.'

'No, I didn't *want* to get married,' Gaetano contradicted drily. 'I've seen too many of my friends' marriages failing and my own parents fought like cat and dog.'

Poppy grimaced and said nothing. Gaetano was very literal, very black and white and uncompromising in his outlook. He had probably decided as a teenager that he would not get married and had never revisited the decision. But it did go some way towards explaining why he never seemed to stay very long with any woman because clearly none of his relationships had had the option of a future.

'At some stage you must have met at least *one* woman who stood out from the rest?' she commented.

'I did…when I was at university. Serena ended up marrying a friend and I was their best man. They divorced last year,' Gaetano volunteered with rich scorn. 'When I heard about that, I was relieved I had backed off from her.'

'That's very cold and cynical. For all you know

you and she could have made a success of marriage,' Poppy commented tongue in cheek, mad with curiosity to know who Serena had been and whether he still had feelings for her now that she was free. Her face burned because she was so grateful he had not persevered with the wretched woman. She was just then discovering in consternation that she couldn't bear to think of Gaetano with *any* other woman, let alone married to one. When had she become that sensitive, that possessive of him? She had no right to feel that way and that she did mortified her. Was this some pitiful hangover from her infatuation with him as a teenager?

As she walked into the hall Gaetano pushed the door open into a dimly lit reception room. 'Before I went out I ordered supper for us. I thought you'd be hungry because unless you ate while you were working, you missed dinner.'

She was strangely touched that it had even occurred to Gaetano to consider her well-being. But then Poppy wasn't used to anyone looking out for her. In recent years she had acted as counsellor and carer for her family. Neither her mother nor her brother had ever had the inclination to ask her how she was coping working two jobs or whether she needed anything. Removing her coat, she sank down into a comfy armchair, glancing round at the stylish appointments of the spacious room. An interior designer had probably been employed, she suspected, doubting that such classy chic was attainable in any other way. She poured the tea and filled her plate with sandwiches.

For a few minutes she simply ate to satisfy the gnawing hunger inside her. Only slowly did she let her attention roam back to Gaetano. The black stubble framed his jaw, accentuating the lush curve of his full mouth, and he could work magic with that mouth, she conceded, inwardly squirming at that intimate thought and the longing behind it while ducking her head to evade the cool gold intensity of his gaze. Her body, still taut and tender from feverish arousal, recalled the stroke of his fingers and she tingled, dying inside with chagrin that she had lost her control to that extent.

'So, what do you want to talk about?' she prompted in the humming silence.

'I think you already know,' Gaetano intoned very drily.

'You have to decide what to do next,' Poppy clarified reluctantly, disliking the fact that he read her with such accuracy and refused to allow her to play dumb when it suited her to do so.

After all, so much hung on the coming discussion and it was only natural that she should now be nervous. Of what further use could she be to Gaetano? Their fake engagement was worthless because Rodolfo Leonetti wanted much more than a fake couple could possibly deliver. They couldn't set a wedding date because they weren't going to get married. And if she was of no additional value to Gaetano, maybe he wanted her to leave his home and maybe, quite understandably, he would also expect to immediately stop paying the bills for her mother's treatment at the clinic? A cold trickle of nervous perspiration ran down between Poppy's breasts and suddenly she was furious with herself for not thinking through what Rodolfo's declaration would ultimately mean to her and the lives of those who depended on her.

'I had no problem deciding what to do next. I'm very decisive but unfortunately what I do next is heavily dependent on what you decide to do,' Gaetano admitted quietly, disconcerting her while his extraordinarily beautiful eyes rested on her full force.

'What *I* decide...?'

'Only a fake fiancée can become a fake bride!' Gaetano derided, watching her pale.

'You can't seriously be suggesting that we carry this masquerade as far as a wedding!' Poppy exclaimed with a look of disbelief.

'Rodolfo likes you. He's really excited and happy about our relationship,' Gaetano breathed grimly. 'In fact it's many years since I saw him this enthusiastic about anything or anyone. I would like to give him what he wants even if it's not real and even though it can't last.'

'You love your grandfather. I understand that you don't want to disappoint him, but—'

'We could get married for a couple of years while I continue to pay for your mother's care.'

Poppy leant forward to say sharply, 'If Mum does well, she will probably be released from the clinic next month.'

Gaetano shook his handsome dark head slowly as if in wonder at her naivety. 'Poppy…Jasmine is most probably a long-term rehabilitation project. To stay off alcohol for the foreseeable future she's going to need regular ongoing professional support.'

It was true, Poppy conceded painfully. What Gaetano was saying was true, *horribly* true, but until that moment Poppy had not thought that far ahead. Indeed she had dreamt only of the day when she hoped and prayed that her newly sober parent would walk out of the clinic and back into the real world. Sadly, however, the real world offered challenges Jasmine Arnold might struggle to handle. And Poppy already knew that she did not have the power to stop her mother drinking because she had already tried that and had failed abysmally.

'If you agree to marry me I will faithfully promise to take care of your mother's needs for however long it takes for her to regain her health and sobriety,' Gaetano swore. 'At the same time I will make it possible for you to return to further education. That would mean that by the time we divorce you would be in a position to pursue any career you chose.'

Poppy sucked in a steadying breath because he was offering to deliver momentous benefits and security. But she still didn't want to sell herself out for the money that would empower her to transform her mother's life and give them both the best possible chance of a decent future. 'I can't take your money or your support. It's immoral,' she argued jaggedly. 'Stop trying to tempt me into doing what I know would be wrong.'

'I'm offering you the equivalent of a job. All right...' Gaetano shifted an expressive bronzed hand in the air with the fluid arrogance that came as naturally as breathing to him. 'Taking on the role of being my wife would be an unusual job but it's not a job you *want*, so why shouldn't you be paid for sacrificing your freedom? Because make no mistake—you *would* be giving up your freedom while you were pretending to be my wife.'

'Fooling your grandfather, faking and pretending. It wouldn't be right,' Poppy protested vehemently.

'If it makes Rodolfo genuinely happy, why is it wrong?' Gaetano fired back at her in challenge. 'It's the best I've got to offer him. I can't give him the real thing. I can't give him a real marriage when I don't want one. Marrying you, a woman he has readily accepted and approved, is as good as it's likely to get from his point of view.'

Poppy was pale and troubled. 'You're good

in an argument,' she allowed ruefully. 'But I'm never going to win a trophy for my acting skills.'

'You don't need to act. Rodolfo likes you as you are. Think about what I'm offering you. You can reclaim your life and return to being a carefree student,' Gaetano pointed out, his persuasion insidious. 'No more fretting about your mother falling off the wagon again, no more scrubbing floors or serving drinks.'

'Shut up!' Poppy told him curtly, leaping to her feet to walk restively round the room while she battled the tempting possibilities he had placed in front of her.

Gaetano studied her from below heavily lashed eyelids. She would surrender, of course she would. She had had a very tough time coping with her mother over the past couple of years and it had stolen her youthful freedom of choice. As a teenager she had been ambitious and he could still see that spirited spark of wanting more than her servant ancestors had ever wanted glowing within her.

'And how long would this fake marriage have to last to be worthwhile?' she demanded without warning.

Gaetano almost grinned and punched the air because that was when he knew for sure that he had won. 'I estimate around two years with three years being the absolute maximum. By that stage both of us will be eager to reclaim our real lives and I would envisage that divorce proceedings would already have begun.'

'And you think a divorce a couple of years down the road is less of a disappointment for Rodolfo than a broken engagement?'

'At least he'll believe I *tried*.'

'And of course your ultimate goal is becoming CEO of the Leonetti Bank and marrying me will deliver that,' Poppy filled in slowly, luminous green eyes skimming to his lean, darkly handsome features in wonderment. 'I can't believe how ambitious you are.'

'The bank is my life, it always has been,'

Gaetano admitted without apology. 'Nothing gives me as much of a buzz as a profitable deal.'

'If I were to agree to this…and I'm not saying I *am* agreeing,' Poppy warned in a rush, 'when would the marriage take place?'

'Next month to suit Rodolfo's schedule and, for that matter, my own. I won't be here much over the next few weeks,' Gaetano explained. 'I have a lot of pressing business to tie up before I can take the kind of honeymoon which Rodolfo will expect.'

At that disconcerting reference to a honeymoon a tension headache tightened in a band across Poppy's brow and she lifted her fingers to press against her forehead. 'I'm very tired. I'll sleep on this and give you an answer in the morning.'

Gaetano slid fluidly out of his seat and approached her. 'But you already know the answer.'

Poppy settled angry green eyes on his lean, strong face. 'Don't try to railroad me,' she warned him.

'You like what I do to you,' Gaetano husked

with blazing confidence, running a teasing fore-finger down over her cheek to stroke it along the soft curve of her full lower lip.

In all her life Poppy had never been more aware of anything than she was of that finger caress-ing the still-swollen surface of her mouth. But then, as she was learning, Gaetano couldn't touch any part of her body without every nerve ending standing to attention and screaming for more of the same. Her breathing fractured in her throat and sawed heavily in and out of her chest. His fingertip slid into her mouth and before she could even think about what she was doing she laved it with her tongue, sucked it, watched his bril-liant eyes smoulder and then his outrageous long black lashes lower over burning glints of gold.

'Are you offering to let me have you tonight?' Gaetano enquired, startling and mortifying her with that direct question.

Her luminous eyes flew wide. 'I can't believe you just asked me that!'

'And I can't believe that you can still try to act

the innocent when you're teasing me,' Gaetano riposted.

'You touched me first,' she reminded him defensively, her cheeks scarlet as she thought of what she had done with his finger and the expectation he had developed as a result. 'Are you always this blunt?'

'Pretty much. Sex requires mutual consent and I naturally dislike confusing signals, which could lead to misunderstandings.'

Poppy stared up at him, momentarily lost in the tawny blaze of his hot stare. He wanted her and he was letting her see it. Her whole body seized up in response, her nipples prickling while that painful hollow ached at the heart of her. She tore her gaze from his, dropped her eyes and then, noticing the sizeable bulge in his jeans, felt pure unashamed heat curling up between her thighs.

'If you're not going to let me have you, sleep in one of the spare rooms tonight,' Gaetano instructed. 'I'm not a masochist, *bella mia*.'

'Spare room,' Poppy framed shakily, the only

words she could get past her tight throat because it hurt her that she wanted to say yes so badly. She didn't want to be used 'to scratch an itch', not her first time anyway. Surely some day somewhere some man would want her for more than that? Gaetano only wanted the release of sex and would probably not have wanted her at all had they not been forced into such proximity.

Gaetano let her reach the door. 'If I marry you, I'll expect you to share my bed.'

Wide-eyed, Poppy whirled round to gasp, 'But...'

'I'm too well-known to get away with sneaking around having affairs for a couple of years,' Gaetano asserted silkily. 'If we get married it should look like a happy marriage, at least at the start, and there's no way I'd be happy in a sex-free marriage. Is that likely to be a deal-breaker?'

'I'll think it over.' Her heart-shaped face expressionless, Poppy studied the polished floor. She wanted to discover sex with Gaetano but she wasn't about to confess that to him. *That* was private, strictly private. Her body burned inside her clothing at the thought of that intimacy. Meaningless, sexual intimacy, she reminded herself doggedly. And it disturbed her that even though she knew it would mean nothing to him she still wanted him...

CHAPTER SIX

POPPY SANK INTO the guest-room bed and rolled over to hug a pillow. She was incredibly tired but so wired she was convinced that she would not sleep a wink.

She was going to marry Gaetano Leonetti. Gorgeous, filthy rich, super-successful Gaetano. Who sent her body into spasms of craving with a single kiss. If she was honest with herself, she really hadn't needed a night to think it over. He would help her protect her mother and he would support her getting back onto a career path. Really, marrying Gaetano would be win-win whichever way she looked at it, wouldn't it be?

As long as she didn't get too carried away and start acting as if it were a real marriage. As long as she didn't fall for Gaetano. Well, she wasn't about to do that, was she? He was almost thirty years old and had never been in love. The closest he had come to love was with a woman who had married his friend. And he had acted as best man at their wedding, which didn't suggest to her that it had been very close to love at all. Gaetano might be planning to marry her but he wasn't going to love her and he wasn't going to keep her either. It would be a temporary marriage and it would make Rodolfo happy...at least for a while, she thought guiltily, because faking it for the older man's benefit still troubled her conscience. He was such a kind, genuine sort of man and so unlike Gaetano, who kept the equivalent of a coffin lid slammed down hard on his emotions.

While Poppy was ruminating over her bridegroom's lack of emotional intelligence, Gaetano was subjecting himself to yet another cold shower. She *had* to marry him. There was no alternative. Just at that moment in the grip of a raging inferno of frustrated lust he felt as though he would spontaneously combust if he didn't get Poppy spread across his bed as the perfect wedding gift. The definitive wedding gift, with those ballerina legs in lace stockings, those pert little breasts in satin cups, that voluptuous pink mouth pouting as she looked up at him with those witchy green spellbinding eyes. He groaned out loud. He couldn't credit that he had barely touched her when he wanted so much more.

But if they married, a few weeks down the matrimonial road he'd be back to normal, he told himself bracingly. The challenge would be gone. The lust would die once he could have her whenever he wanted her. He would soon be himself again, cooler, calmer, back in control, fully focussed on the bank. How was it possible that just the fantasy of sinking into Poppy's wet, willing body excited him more than he had ever been excited? What was it about her?

Maybe it was the weird clothes, maybe he had a secret Goth fetish. Maybe it was her argumentative nature, because he had always thrilled to a challenge. Maybe it was her cheeky texts that made him laugh. The fact she could still blush? That was strange. Every time he mentioned sex she went red, as if he had said something outrageous. She couldn't possibly be that innocent, although he was willing to allow that she might well have considerably less experience between the sheets than he had acquired.

Gaetano shook Poppy awake at the ungodly hour of six in the morning, obstinately and cruelly ignoring her heartfelt moans to insist that she join him for breakfast. After a quick shower and the application of a little make-up, Poppy teamed a black dress enlivened with a red rose print with high heels and sauntered down to the dining room. Gaetano was already ensconced with black coffee, a horrendously unhealthy fry-up and the *Financial Times*.

She was gloriously conscious of his attention as she helped herself to cereal and took a seat at the other end of the table, her ruby cluster ring catching the light. Gaetano put down the newspaper and regarded her levelly, dark golden eyes steady as a rock and full of an impatience he didn't need to voice.

'Yes, I'll marry you,' Poppy told him straight off.

'Does that mean I get to share my bed with you tonight?' was Gaetano's first telling question.

'You are incredibly goal-orientated about entirely the wrong things!' Poppy censured immediately. 'You can wait until we're married.'

'Nobody waits until they're married these days!'

'I haven't had sex before. I want it to feel special,' she told him stubbornly.

His expressive dark eyes flared with incredulity. 'I refuse to credit that. I saw you with Toby Styles…'

'I hate you!' Poppy launched at him in a sudden tempest of furious embarrassment, her pale skin flushed to her hairline. 'Of all the moments I don't *want* to be reminded of, you have to bring that one up and throw it at me!'

'Well, it was one of those unforgettable moments that did seem fairly self-explanatory. I saw you sidling out of the shrubbery covered in blushes and grass stains,' Gaetano commented with grudging amusement. 'So, why lie about it? This is purely about sex, *bella mia*, and I'm all for full bedroom equality. Whether or not you're a virgin or a secret slut matters not a damn to me.'

Poppy compressed her lips. 'If you must know—although it's none of your blasted business—I did plan to have sex that day with Toby but I changed my mind because it wasn't what I really wanted.' No, what she had really, *really* wanted that day, she acknowledged belatedly, was to wander off into the shrubbery and be ravished by Gaetano, who had dominated her every juvenile fantasy. Sadly, however, Gaetano hadn't been an option.

'Poor Toby...' Gaetano frowned.

'He was very decent about it,' Poppy muttered in mortification. 'He's married to one of my friends now.'

'But there must have been someone since then?'

'No.'

Gaetano continued to stare at her as if she were a circus freak. 'But you're so full of passion...'

Only with you. The words remained unspoken.

Gaetano lifted his coffee with a slightly dazed expression in his shrewd gaze. 'I'll be the first... *really*?'

Poppy shrugged a shoulder. 'But if you think it's likely to be a turn-off I can always go and look for a one-night stand.'

'Don't even think about it,' Gaetano growled.

'That was a joke.'

'It's not a turn-off, simply a surprise,' Gaetano admitted flatly. 'OK, I'll wait until we're married if it's so significant to you. But I think you're making an unnecessary production out of it.'

Her body was all he wanted from her, Poppy interpreted painfully. At least if she was his legal wife, it would feel less demeaning, wouldn't it?

'I'll organise a gynae appointment for you,' Gaetano continued briskly. 'Reliable birth control is important. We don't want any slip-ups in that department when we're not planning to stay together.'

'Obviously not,' she agreed, sipping with determination at her hot-chocolate drink while thinking for the very first time in her life about having a baby. She had always liked children, always assumed that she would become a mother one day, but she reckoned that day lay a long way ahead in her future.

'And whatever you do,' Gaetano warned with chilling precision, 'don't go falling for me.'

'And why would I do that?' Poppy demanded baldly, her cheeks hotter than hell in fear of him mentioning that so mortifying teenaged crush again. 'Having sex with you is not going to make me fall in love with you. I know you think you're fantastic in bed, Gaetano, *but* you're not fantastic enough *out* of bed.'

Infuriatingly, Gaetano did not react badly to that criticism. 'That's good because that's one complication I can do without. I hate it when women fall for me and make me feel that it's my fault.'

Well, that was frank, and forewarned was fore-armed, Poppy told herself squarely. 'It's probably your money they're falling for,' she suggested in a tone of saccharine sweetness. 'You have yet to show me a single loveable trait.'

'*Grazie al cielo*...thank goodness,' Gaetano responded in a tone of galling relief. 'I don't want you to get the wrong idea about me *or* this marriage.'

'I won't. This marriage will be like one of those business mergers. You are *so* safe,' Poppy declared brightly. 'You will merely be the first stepping stone on my sexual path.'

Gaetano was taken aback to discover that he didn't want to think of a string of other men enjoying her along that particular path. In fact it gave him a slightly nauseated sensation in the pit of his stomach. The acknowledgement bemused him and he put it down to the simple fact that as yet he had not enjoyed her either. He was thinking too much about something relatively unimportant, he reflected impatiently. Sex was sex and his wedding night would provide the cure for what was currently afflicting him. Since when had he ever attached so much consequence to sex? Even so, it had been entirely right to have the conversation with Poppy to ensure that they perfectly understood each other's expectations.

'I'll make a start on the wedding arrangements today,' Gaetano completed smoothly.

'You look beautiful,' Jasmine Arnold told her daughter warmly as she emerged from her bedroom in her wedding dress.

The older woman was attending her daughter's wedding with a member of the clinic support staff. Although Poppy could see a big improvement in her mother's appearance and mood, she knew how hard it was for Jasmine to return to Woodfield Hall where she had been so depressed. And while Poppy had asked her mother to walk her down the aisle, her brother was doing it instead because Jasmine could not face being the centre of that much attention.

Poppy quite understood the older woman's reluctance because hundreds of guests were attending the wedding being staged to celebrate Gaetano's marriage at Woodfield Hall. The Leonetti men had always got married in the church in the grounds of their ancestral home and neither Rodolfo nor Gaetano had seen any reason to flout tradition. Indeed Gaetano had expected Poppy to move straight into the main house as though she already belonged there but Poppy had returned to the small service flat where she had grown up, determined to move back and forth as required.

'I'm still hoping that you know what you're doing,' Damien muttered in an admission intended only for Poppy's ears as he emerged from his own room, smartly clad in his hired morning suit. He looked relieved when he registered that his mother and her companion had already left for the church. 'You've always had a thing for Gaetano...'

'As I've already explained, this is only a business arrangement.'

'Maybe it is...for him.' Her brother sighed. 'But if it's only business why are you always checking your phone and texting him?'

'He expects regular updates on the wedding arrangements.'

'Yeah...like his staff can't do that for him,' Damien responded, unimpressed.

But it was true, Poppy reflected ruefully. Gaetano was hyper about details and had a surprising number of strong opinions about bridal matters that she had mistakenly assumed he wouldn't be interested in. Although, as he had warned her, she had barely seen him since the month-long countdown to the wedding had begun, they had stayed in constant contact by phone while Gaetano flew round Europe. Poppy had ignored his opinion of the casual job she had taken and had kept up regular shifts at the café.

Now she climbed into the limousine waiting in the courtyard to collect the bride and her brother. The chapel was barely two hundred yards away and she would have much preferred to walk there but Gaetano had vetoed that option, saying it lacked dignity.

In the same way he had vetoed the flowers she'd wanted to wear in her hair and had had a family diamond tiara delivered to her. He had also picked the bridal colour scheme as green, arguing that that particular shade would match her eyes, which had struck Poppy as ridiculously whimsical for so practical a male. And to crown his interference he had acted as though he were her Prince Charming by buying her wedding shoes the instant he saw them showcased in some high-fashion outlet in Milan. Admittedly they were gorgeous, even if they were over-the-top dramatic—delicate leather sandals ornamented with pearls and opals that glimmered and magically shone in the light. In fact Gaetano had embarrassed his bride with his choice of shoes because her selections had been considerably less fanciful. Her dress was cap-sleeved and fitted to the waist, flaring out over net underskirts to stop above her slender knees. In comparison to the Cinderella shoes, the dress, while being composed of beautiful fabric, was plain and simple in style.

'Are you nervous?' Damien prompted.

'Why would I be? Well, only because the Leonettis have invited hundreds of people,' she admitted.

'Including most of the estate staff and locals, so you can't fault Gaetano there. The rich are going to have to rub shoulders with the ordinary folk.' Damien laughed.

Poppy smiled because Gaetano had kept the last promise he had made before their engagement. Within a week Damien would be starting work as a mechanic in a London garage staffed by other former offenders. Her brother's happiness at the prospect of a complete new start somewhere he would no longer be pilloried for his past had lifted her heart. Not that her heart needed lifting, she told herself urgently. If her family was happy, *she* was happy. In stray moments between the wedding arrangements and spending time with Rodolfo, who got lonely in his big empty mansion, she had started looking into the option of training as a garden designer and that gem of an idea looked promising.

Closing her hand into the crook of her brother's arm, she looked down the aisle to where Gaetano had turned round to see her arrival and she grinned. My goodness, how ridiculous all this pomp and ceremony were for a couple who weren't remotely in love, she thought helplessly. But Gaetano certainly looked the part of bridegroom, all tall, dark and handsome, black curls cropped to his head in honour of the wedding, the usual stubble round his jaw line dispensed with, his bronzed, handsome features clean-shaven. His dark eyes glittered gold as precious ingots in the sunlight filtered by the stained-glass window behind him. He looked downright amazing, she conceded with a sunny sensation of absolute contentment.

When Poppy came into view, she took Gaetano's breath away. Her waist looked tiny enough to be spanned by his hands and, as he had requested, her glorious hair tumbled loose round her shoulders in vibrant contrast to the white dress that displayed her incredible legs. And she was wearing the shoes, the shoes *he* had bought for her, having known at a glance and feeling slightly smug at the knowledge that they were the sort of theatrical feminine touch the unconventional Poppy would appreciate.

The priest rattled through the ceremony at a fair old pace. Rings were exchanged. Poppy trembled as Gaetano eased the ring down over her knuckle, glancing up to encounter smouldering golden eyes that devoured her. Colour surged into her face as she thought of the night ahead but there was anticipation and excitement laced with that faint sense of apprehension. She had decided that she was glad that Gaetano would become her first lover. Who better than the male she had fallen for as a teenager? After all, no other man had yet managed to wipe out her memory of Gaetano. There would be someone else some day, she told herself bracingly as Gaetano retained her hand and his thumb gently massaged the delicate skin of her inner wrist with the understated sensuality that seemed so much a part of him.

'You made me wait ten minutes at the altar but you were definitely worth waiting for,' Gaetano quipped as they walked down the aisle again.

'I warned you I'd be late,' Poppy reminded him. 'Knowing you, you'd have preferred to find me waiting humbly for you.'

'No, waiting naked would have been sufficient, late or otherwise,' Gaetano whispered only loud enough for her ears. 'As for humble—are you kidding? You've never been the self-effacing type.'

Rodolfo hugged her outside the chapel, his creased face wrinkled into a huge smile. 'Welcome to the family,' he said happily.

A beautiful blonde watched with raised brows of apparent surprise as, urged on by the photographer, Poppy wound her arms round Gaetano's neck and gazed at him as if he were her sun, her moon and her stars. She was great at faking it, she thought appreciatively as Gaetano smiled down at her with that wonderful, charismatic smile that banished the often forbidding austerity from his lean, darkly handsome features.

'Congratulations, Gaetano,' the blonde intercepted them as they made their way to the limo to be wafted back to the hall.

'Poppy…meet Serena Bellingham. We'll catch up later, Serena,' Gaetano drawled.

'Is she the one you almost married?' Poppy demanded, craning her neck to look back at the smiling blonde who rejoiced in the height, perfect figure and face of a top model.

'Oh, don't do it. Don't make something out of nothing the way women do!' Gaetano groaned in exasperation. 'I didn't *almost* marry Serena and, even if I did, what business is it of yours? This isn't a real wedding.'

The colour ebbed from below Poppy's skin to leave her pale. She felt oddly as though she had been slapped down and squashed and she felt enormously hurt and humiliated but didn't understand why. But, unquestionably, he was right. Theirs was not a normal wedding and she was not entitled to ask nosy personal questions about exes.

As if he recognised that he had been rude, Gaetano released his breath in a slow measured hiss. 'I'm sorry. I shouldn't have said that.'

'No, it's OK. I'm just naturally nosy,' Poppy muttered in an undertone.

'Serena is a very talented hedge-fund manager. She may come and work for Leonettis now that she's single again. Her ex was envious of her success, which is—apparently—the main reason their marriage failed.'

Poppy pictured Serena's cloyingly bright smile and her tummy performed a warning somersault.

It sounded as though Gaetano had spoken to Serena recently to catch up. Confidences had been exchanged and that sent the oddest little current of dismay through Poppy. She suspected that if the beautiful blonde went to work for Gaetano, it wouldn't entirely be a career move. But even if that was true, what business was it of hers to judge or speculate? She was Gaetano's wife and soon she would also be Gaetano's lover yet she had not, it seemed, acquired any relationship rights over Gaetano, which suddenly struck her as a recipe for disaster.

Woodfield Hall was awash with guests and caterers. Jasmine Arnold approached her daughter to ask if it would be all right if she took her leave. Newly sober, Poppy's mother did not want as yet to be in the vicinity of alcohol. Understanding, Poppy hugged the older woman and they agreed to talk regularly on the phone. As Gaetano joined her Poppy smiled at one of her few school friends, Melanie, who was now married to Toby Styles, the estate gamekeeper.

Overpowered by Gaetano's presence, the small brunette gushed into speech. 'You and…er…Mr Leonetti? It's so romantic, Poppy. You know,' Melanie said, addressing Gaetano directly, 'the whole time we were growing up Poppy never had eyes for anyone but you.'

Gaetano responded wittily but Poppy was already trying not to cringe before Toby grinned at her. 'Nobody knows that better than me,' he teased.

Kill me now, Poppy thought melodramatically when Gaetano actually laughed out loud and chatted to the couple about their work on the estate as if nothing the slightest bit embarrassing had been shared. And of course, why would it embarrass Gaetano to be reminded of Poppy's adolescent crush?

As they mingled she noticed Rodolfo chatting to Serena Bellingham. The blonde was wreathed in charming smiles. Poppy scolded herself for thinking bitchy thoughts. And why? Just because Serena had once shared a bed with Gaetano? Just because Serena had the looks, the social background and the education that would have made her the perfect wife for Gaetano? Or because Gaetano had once freely chosen to have a relationship with Serena when he had merely ended up with Poppy by accident and retained her for convenience?

Deliberately catching her eye, Serena strolled over to Poppy's side. 'I can see that you're curious about me,' she drawled in her cut-glass accent. 'I'm Gaetano's only serious ex, so it's natural...'

'Possibly,' Poppy conceded, determined to be very cautious with her words and ashamed of the explosive mixture of inexcusable envy and resentment she was struggling to suppress.

'We were too young when we first met,' Serena declared. 'That's why we broke up. Gaetano wasn't ready to commit and I was, so I rushed off and married someone else instead.'

'Everyone matures at a different rate,' Poppy remarked non-committally.

'Maturity is immaterial,' Serena responded

with stinging confidence. 'You and Gaetano won't last five minutes. You don't have anything to offer him.'

Disconcerted by that sudden attack coming at her out of nowhere, Poppy froze. 'That's a matter of opinion.'

'But you'll do very well for a short-lived *first* marriage. Gaetano is the last man alive I would expect to stay married to a Goth bride. You don't fit in and you never will...'

As that bitingly cold forecast hit her Poppy was silenced by Gaetano's arm closing round her spine. She encountered a suspicious sidewise glance and her temper flared inside her. Evidently, Gaetano was so far removed from the reality of Serena's barracuda nature that it was Poppy he didn't trust to behave around Serena. Entrapped there in Gaetano's controlling hold, Poppy silently seethed and brooded over what Serena had said.

Sadly, the blonde's assurance that Poppy would never fit in as Gaetano's wife had cut deep—particularly because Poppy had quite deliberately made conventional choices when it came to what to wear for her wedding day. Why had she done that? she suddenly asked herself angrily. And there it was—the answer she didn't want. She had done it for Gaetano's benefit in an effort to please him and make him proud of her, make him appreciate that the housekeeper's daughter could get it right for a big occasion. Serena's automatic dismissal of all that Poppy had to offer had seriously hurt and humiliated her.

Fortunately from that point on their wedding day seemed to speed up and race past. Poppy's throat was sore and she put that down to the amount of talking she had to do. She ate little during the meal even though she was trying to regain the weight she had lost in recent months while she had worked two jobs. Unfortunately her appetite had vanished.

She changed into white cropped trousers and a cool blue chiffon top for their flight to Italy. The luxurious interior of the Leonetti private jet stunned her into silence. She studied the glittering ruby cluster nestling next to the wedding band on her finger and Serena's wounding forecast of her marriage seemed to reverberate in her ears. *You don't fit in and you never will.*

And why should that matter when they didn't plan to stay married? Poppy asked herself wearily, unsettled by the nagging insecurities tugging at her. Why should she care what Serena thought? Or what Serena truly wanted from Gaetano? She reckoned that Serena was already planning to be Gaetano's second, rather more permanent wife. So what?

It wasn't as though she had any feelings for Gaetano beyond tolerance, Poppy reminded herself. Lust was physical, not cerebral.

CHAPTER SEVEN

'*STOP... STOP THE CAR!*' Poppy yelled as the Range Rover wound down the twisting Tuscan country road.

Startled, Gaetano jumped on the brake. He frowned in astonishment as Poppy leapt out of the car at speed and assumed that she felt sick. But to his surprise and that of the security men climbing out of the car behind, Poppy ran back down the road and crouched down.

Bloodstains and dust had smeared her white cropped jeans by the time she stood up again cradling something hairy and still in her arms as tenderly as if it were a baby. 'It's a dog...it must've been hit by a passing car.'

'Give it to my security. They'll deal with this,' Gaetano advised.

'No, we will,' Poppy told him. 'Where's the closest veterinary surgery?'

The dog, a terrier mix with a pepper and salt coat and a greying snout, licked weakly at her fingers and whined in pain. Fifteen minutes later they were in the waiting room at the local surgery while Gaetano spoke with the vet in Italian.

'The situation is this...' Gaetano informed Poppy. 'The animal is not microchipped, has no collar and has not been reported missing. Arno can operate and I can obviously afford to cover the cost of the treatment but it may be more practical simply to put the animal to sleep.'

'Practical?' Poppy erupted.

'Rather than put the dog through the trauma of surgery and a prolonged recuperation when the local pound is already full, as is the animal rescue sanctuary. If there is no prospect of the dog going to another home—'

'I'll keep him,' Poppy cut in curtly.

Gaetano groaned. 'Don't be a bleeding heart for the sake of it.'

'I'm not. I *want* Muffin.'

His gorgeous dark eyes widened in surprise, black lashes sky-high. *'Muffin?'*

'Ragamuffin… Muffin,' she explained curtly.

'But I can buy you a beautiful pedigreed puppy if you want one,' Gaetano murmured with unconcealed incredulity. 'Muffin is no oil painting and he's old.'

'So? He needs me much more than a beautiful puppy ever would,' Poppy pointed out defiantly. 'Think of him as a wedding gift.'

Having made arrangements for Muffin's care, they drove off again.

'You've become so cold-hearted,' Poppy whispered ruefully, studying his lean dark classic profile. 'What happened to you?'

'I grew up. Don't be a drama queen,' Gaetano urged. 'When you care too much you get hurt. I learned that from a young age.'

'But you're shutting yourself off from so many good things in life,' she argued.

'Am I? Rodolfo enjoyed a long and happy marriage but he was so wretched after my grand-mother passed that he too wanted to die.'

'That was grief. Think of all the happy years he enjoyed with his wife,' Poppy urged. 'Every-thing has a downside, Gaetano. Love brings its own reward.'

Gaetano voiced a single rude word of disagree-ment in Italian. 'It didn't reward my mother when the husband she once adored ran round snort-ing cocaine with hookers. It didn't reward me as her son when her super-rich second husband per-suaded her to forget that she had left a child be-hind in England. But you'll be glad to know that my mother's second husband *loved* her,' Gaetano continued with raw derision. 'As she explained when she tried to foolishly mend fences with me a few years ago, Connor loved her so much that he was jealous of her first marriage and the child born from it.'

Poppy had paled. 'That's a twisted kind of love.'

'And there's a lot of that twisted stuff out there,' Gaetano completed in a chilling tone of finality.

'That's why I never wanted anything to do with that kind of emotion.'

Poppy knew when to keep quiet. Of course, his outlook was coloured by his background, she reflected ruefully. Her parents had been happily married but his had not been. And his mother's decision to turn her back on her son to please her second husband had done even more damage. Poppy had been surprised that Gaetano's mother had not been invited to the wedding but Rodolfo had simply shrugged, saying only that his former daughter-in-law rarely returned to England.

Gaetano turned off the winding road onto a lane that threaded through silvery olive groves. Woods lay beyond the groves, occasionally parting to show views of rolling green hills and vineyards and an ancient walled hilltop village. Gaetano indicated another track to the left. 'That leads down to the guest house where Rodolfo spends his summers.'

'We'll have to be careful to stay in role with

your grandfather staying so close,' Poppy re-marked.

'La Fattoria, the main house, is over a mile away. He won't see us unless we visit. He is very keen not to intrude in any way on what he regards as our honeymoon,' Gaetano said drily.

'So this property has belonged to your family for a long time,' she assumed.

'Rodolfo bought it before I was born, fondly picturing it as the perfect spot for wholesome family holidays with at least half a dozen chil-dren running round.' Gaetano sounded regretful on the older man's behalf rather than scornful. 'Sadly I was an only child and my parents only ever came here with parties of friends. The house was signed over to me about five years ago and I had it fully renovated.'

A magnificent building composed of creamy stone appeared round the next corner. It was larger than Poppy had expected but she was learning to think big or bigger when it came to Leonetti properties, for, while the family might only consist of Rodolfo and his one grandson, the older man did not seem to think in terms of small or convenient. Glorious urns of flowers adorned the terrace and a rotund little woman in an apron, closely followed by a tall lanky man, appeared at the front door.

'Dolores and Sean look after La Fattoria.' Gaetano introduced the friendly middle-aged Irish couple and their cases were swept away.

Poppy accepted a glass of wine and sat down on the rear terrace to enjoy the stupendous view and catch her breath in the sweltering heat. She was feeling incredibly tired and had tactfully declined Dolores's invitation to do an immediate tour of the house. Worse still, she was getting a headache and she had an annoying tickle in her sore throat that had made her cough several times and was giving her voice a rough edge. It was just her luck, she thought ruefully. She was on her honeymoon in Tuscany in the most gorgeous setting, with an even more gorgeous man, and she was developing a galloping bad cold.

* * *

The master bedroom was a huge airy space with a tiled floor and a bed as big as a football pitch. The bathroom was fitted out like a glossy magazine spread and she revelled in the wet room with the complex jet system. Everything bore Gaetano's contemporary stamp and the extreme shower facilities were not a surprise. She had been feeling very warm and the cold water gushing over her before she managed to work out how to operate the complicated controls cooled her off wonderfully. Clad in a light cotton sundress, she wandered back downstairs.

Black hair curling and still damp from the shower, Gaetano joined her on the terrace to slot another glass of wine into her hand. 'From our own award-winning winery,' he told her wryly. 'Rodolfo takes a personal interest in the vineyard.'

Poppy surveyed him from below her lashes. He was so beautiful, she found it a challenge to look anywhere else. His spectacular black-

lashed eyes were reflective as he leant grace-
fully up against a stone pillar support to survey
the panoramic landscape, his lithe, lean, powerful body indolently relaxed. A faint shadow of
black stubble roughened his strong jaw line, accentuating the wide sensual curve of his mouth.
A tiny nerve snaked tight somewhere in her pelvis as she thought of how long it had been since
he kissed her and whether a kiss could possibly
be as unbelievably good as she remembered it
being. Likely not, she told herself, for she had
always been a dreamer. How else could she
have imagined even as a teenager that Gaetano
Leonetti would ever be seriously interested in
her?

And yet, here she was, a little voice whispered
seductively, Gaetano's wedding ring on her finger, and mortifyingly that awareness went to her
head like the strongest alcohol. But their marriage still wasn't real; it was *still* a fantasy, the
same little voice added. She had been a fake fiancée and a fake bride and now she was a fake wife.

In fact just about the only thing that wouldn't be fake between them was their wedding night.

The very blood in her veins seemed to be coursing slowly, heavily. She finished her wine and set down the glass, insanely aware of the tightening prominence of her nipples. She lifted the tiny handwritten menu displayed on the table, glancing with a sinking heart through the several courses that were to be served.

'You know, I'm not remotely hungry and I don't think I *could* eat anything,' Poppy confided truthfully. 'I hope that's not going to offend Dolores…'

Gaetano glanced at her, eyes flaming golden as a lion's in the sunset lighting up the sky in an awesome display of crimson and peach. Mouth suddenly dry, she stopped breathing, frowning as he strode back into the house and disappeared from view. A few minutes later she heard a noisy little car start up somewhere and drive away. Gaetano reappeared to close a hand over hers and tug her gently back indoors.

'Do we have to eat in some stuffy dining room?' She sighed.

'No, we don't have to do anything we don't want to do,' Gaetano told her, bending down to lift her up into his arms. 'I've sent Sean and Dolores home. We're on our own until tomorrow and I am much hungrier for you than for food.'

'You can't possibly carry me up those stairs!' Poppy exclaimed.

'Right at this moment I could carry you up ten flights of stairs, *bellezza mia*,' Gaetano admitted, darting his mouth across her collarbone so that her head fell back to expose her slender white throat and her bright hair cascaded over his arm. 'Congratulations on being the only woman smart enough to make me wait...'

'Wait for what? *Oh*...' Poppy registered with a wealth of meaning in her tone while distinctly revelling in being carried as though she were a little dainty thing, which, in her own opinion, she was not.

Gaetano settled her down on the bed. Helpfully she kicked off her shoes and wished she had taken a painkiller for her sore throat and head. But she couldn't possibly take the gloss off the evening by admitting that she was feeling under par, could she? And she would have to admit it to get medication because she had packed nothing of that nature, indeed had only brought her contraceptive pills with her. She wasn't about to make a fuss about a stupid cold, was she?

He ran down the zip on her dress but only after kissing a path across her bare shoulders and lingering at the nape of her neck where her skin proved to be incredibly sensitive and she quivered, her insides turning to liquid heat beneath his attention.

'I have died and gone to heaven...' Gaetano intoned thickly as the dress dropped unnoticed to the carpet, exposing his bride in her ice-blue satin corset top and matching knickers.

'This is your wedding present,' Poppy announced, stretching back against the smooth white bedding with a confidence that she had never known she could possess.

Of course it would be different once he started removing stuff and nudity got involved, she conceded ruefully. For now, however, having guessed that Gaetano would be the type of male who found sexy lingerie that enhanced a woman's figure appealing, Poppy felt like a million dollars. Why? Simply because somehow Gaetano always contrived to look at her as if she had the most amazing female body ever and that had done wonders for her self-image.

'No, *you* are my wedding present,' Gaetano told her with conviction. 'I've been counting down the hours until we were together.'

Her luminous green eyes widened in surprise and she bit back the tactless retort that anyone would consider that a romantic comment. After all, Gaetano was fully focused on sex and neither romance nor commitment would play any part in their marriage. And wasn't that all she was focused on as well? As Gaetano came down on the bed beside her, his shirt hanging loose and unbuttoned to display a sleek, bronzed, muscular six-pack, Poppy was entranced by the view. He was stunning and, for now, he was hers. Why look beyond that? Why try to complicate things?

Loosening the corset one hook at a time, Gaetano ran a long finger down over the delicate spine he had exposed and then put his mouth there, tracing the line below her smooth ivory skin. 'You are so beautiful, *gioia mia.*'

Poppy hid a blissed-out smile behind her tumbling hair and closed her eyes as he eased off the light corset and lifted his hands to cup her breasts. Her back arched, her straining nipples pushing against his fingers until he tugged on the tender buds and an audible gasp escaped her.

Gaetano lifted her and turned her round to face him. 'I want to be your first,' he breathed in a roughened undertone. 'It will be my privilege.'

'Careful, Gaetano...you're sounding nice.' Now outrageously aware of her naked breasts, Poppy crossed her arms to hide them.

'I may be many things, but nice isn't one of them,' Gaetano growled, pulling her down on the bed beside him and covering her pouting mouth hungrily with his own. Unbridled pleasure snaked through her as his tongue merged with hers. An electrifying push of hunger gripped her as his hands shifted to toy with her breasts. He pushed her back against the pillows and lowered his mouth to her pouting nipples.

'Palest pink like pearls,' Gaetano mused, stroking a tender tip with appreciation as he gazed down at her.' I wondered what colour they would be...'

Her green eyes widened. 'Seriously?' she prompted.

'And they're perfect like the rest of you,' he groaned, lowering his head to lick a distended crest. 'You were so worth waiting for at the church.'

Poppy wasn't quite as pleased as she would have assumed she would be by having that much appreciation directed at her physical attributes.

Gaetano was interfering with her fantasy, that fantasy that she had not even acknowledged was playing at the back of her mind, the fantasy in which Gaetano loved her and appreciated her for all sorts of other reasons that went beyond lust.

'And so were you,' Poppy told Gaetano, deciding to turn the tables as she sat up to dislodge him and pushed him back against the pillows. He studied her with questioning dark golden eyes semi-veiled by black curling lashes. She spread her fingers across his hard pectoral muscles, stroking down over his sleek ribcage to his flat abdomen.

'Don't stop now,' he husked.

Her fingers were clumsy on his belt buckle and the button on the waistband of his trousers, her knuckles nudging against the little furrow of dark hair that disappeared below his clothing. She reached for the zip. Her lack of expertise was obvious to Gaetano and the oddest sensation of tenderness infiltrated him as he noted the tense self-consciousness etched in her flushed face.

'Why do I get the feeling this is a first for you?'

'Everyone is a learner at some stage…' she framed jerkily.

Gaetano yanked down his zip for himself and then tossed her back flat on the bed again while he divested himself of his trousers and his boxers. 'If you touched me now, it would all be over far too fast,' he told her thickly. 'That's why I'm going to do most of the touching and you will lie back and let me do the work.'

'If you think of it as work, I don't think you should bother.'

'Nothing would stop me now. I can hardly wait to be inside you.' Gaetano leant over her, his urgent erection pushing against her hip. 'Having you in my bed has been my fantasy for weeks.'

'Fantasy never lives up to reality,' Poppy said nervously. 'I don't want to be a fantasy.'

'Sorry, it's *my* fantasy,' Gaetano traded, stroking a wondering hand down over the slender curve of her hip to the hot, damp secret at the heart of her.

Her hips jerked and her eyes shut as he traced between her thighs. Her breath snarled in her throat. She was so sensitised that she shuddered when he circled her clitoris with his fingertip. Her whole body was climbing of its own volition into a tight, tense spiral of growing need. Even the brush of a finger against her tight entrance was almost too much to bear. Her hips pushed against the mattress, her heart thumping like thunder inside her chest as he shimmied down the bed, fingertips delicately caressing her inner thighs as he pushed her legs back, opening her.

'No, you can't do that!' she gasped in consternation.

'*Stai zitto...*' he told her softly. 'You don't get to tell me what to do in bed.'

The flick of his tongue across torturously tender nerve endings deprived her of voice and then of thought. Her head shifted back and forth on the pillows, the thrum of hunger building up through her body to a siren's scream of need. She gasped, she cried his name, she moaned, she lost control so completely and utterly that when the explosive release of orgasm claimed her it took her by storm. And the world stopped turning for long minutes, her body still quaking with wondrous aftershocks while Gaetano looked down at her with satisfaction.

As Gaetano tilted her back she felt the smooth steel push of him against her still-throbbing core. The tight knot low in her pelvis made its presence felt again, the hollow ache of hunger stirring afresh. He slid against her, easing into her by degrees, straining her delicate sheath.

'You're so tight,' he groaned, pulling back again and then angling his hips for another, more forceful entrance.

The sharp stinging pain made Poppy flinch for a millisecond and then her body was pushing on past that fleeting discomfort to linger on the satisfying stretch and fullness of his invasion. A little moan broke low in her throat and she moved her hips to luxuriate in the throbbing hardness of his bold masculinity.

Gaetano swore in Italian. 'You feel like heaven,' he growled in her ear. 'Am I hurting you now?'

'Oh, no,' she told him truthfully.

And then he moved again, withdrawing and spearing deep enough to wring a cry of startled enjoyment from her. From that moment on her eagerness climbed in tune with Gaetano's every measured thrust. Her heart raced, her legs clamping round his lean hips as she lifted to him, matching his driving rhythm while the electrifying excitement continued to build. And when she reached that peak for the second time she plunged over it in a fevered delirium of intense quivering release and lay adrift in pleasure.

'That was amazing,' Gaetano muttered thickly, rolling over onto his back while curving an arm round her trembling body. '*You* were amazing, *bella mia.*'

Poppy felt totally exhausted and she was content to lie there in the circle of his arms and marvel at the sublime sense of peace she was experiencing. Belatedly, she acknowledged that her throat and head had now become seriously sore. She hoped that Gaetano wouldn't catch her cold and felt guilty for not warning him.

In fact she was just about to mention her affliction when Gaetano sat up to say quietly, 'Possibly part of the reason it felt so amazing was that it was the very first time I've had sex bareback.'

'Bareback?' she queried.

'I didn't use protection. I had a health check a couple of weeks ago to ensure that I'm clean and you're guarded against pregnancy,' he reminded her. 'I couldn't resist the temptation to try it.'

Poppy made no comment because she knew that he would be ultra-careful with her in the protection stakes because to be careless and risk a pregnancy would come at too high a price for either of them.

'I'm really hungry now...aren't you?' Gaetano admitted, thrusting back the sheet and vacating the bed.

'Not really, no.' Indeed the thought of forcing

food past her aching throat made her wince. 'But I could murder a cup of tea.'

'You'll have to make it for yourself,' he warned her. 'I sent the staff home.'

'I've been making tea for myself since I was a child,' she told him wryly.

'I forgot.' Faint colour enhancing the exotic slant of his cheekbones, Gaetano frowned. 'Your voice sounds funny...'

'I'm getting a cold.' Poppy sighed. 'I hope you don't get it too.'

'I never catch colds.' Gaetano vanished into the bathroom and a moment later she heard the shower running.

Poppy was so exhausted that she really didn't want to move, but exhaustion was something she had become practised at shaking off and working through in recent months when she had spent all day cleaning Woodfield Hall and then had stood at the bar serving drinks all evening. Sliding out of bed, she went into the dressing room to pick an outfit and padded off to find another bathroom to use.

Gaetano hadn't hurt her much, she thought tiredly as she dressed. He had been considerate. He had made it incredibly enjoyable. Why did the knowledge that he had learned how to make sex enjoyable with other women stab her like a knife? She blinked, feeling hot and more than a little dizzy. Clearly she had caught an absolute doozy of a cold but she didn't want to be a burden by admitting to Gaetano that she felt awful. A good night's sleep would make her feel much better.

Casually clad in cotton palazzo pants and a tee shirt, she went downstairs, located the kitchen and put on the kettle. She heard Gaetano talking to someone and her brow pleated as she walked to the doorway to see who it was. She almost groaned out loud when she finally realised that he was talking into his phone in tones that sounded angry. As his brilliant dark golden eyes landed on her she froze at the chilling light in his gaze.

'What's wrong?' she asked, her voice fracturing into roughness.

Gaetano thrust his phone back in the pocket of his jeans and stared at her angrily, almost as if he'd never seen her before. 'That was Rodolfo calling to warn me about something some tabloid newspaper plans to print tomorrow. One of his old friends in the press tipped him off...'

'Oh?' Poppy heard the kettle switching off behind her and turned away, desperate to ease her sore throat with a hot drink.

Gaetano bit out a sharp, unamused laugh. 'When were you planning to tell me that you once worked as a nude model?'

Poppy spun back, wide-eyed with astonishment. 'What on earth are you talking about?'

'That filthy rag is going to print photos of you naked tomorrow. My wife *naked* in a newspaper for the world to see!' Gaetano launched at her in outrage. '*Madonna diavolo*...how could you cheapen yourself like that?'

'I've never worked as a nude model. There

couldn't possibly be photos of me naked any-where...' Poppy protested and then she stilled, literally freezing into place, sudden anxiety fill-ing her eyes.

'Oh, you've just remembered doing it, have you?' Gaetano derided harshly. 'Well, thanks for warning me. If I'd known I would've bought the photos to keep them off the market.'

'It's not like you think,' Poppy began awk-wardly, horrified at the idea that illegal shots might have been taken of her at the photographic studio while she was unaware. But what else could she think?

As something akin to an anxiety attack claimed her already overheated body Poppy found it very hard to catch her breath. She dropped dizzily down into the chair by the scrubbed pine table. 'I'm not feeling well,' she mumbled apologeti-cally.

'If you think that feigning illness is likely to get you out of this particular tight corner, it's not,' Gaetano asserted in such a temper that he could hardly keep his voice level and his volume under control.

The mere idea of nude photos of Poppy being splashed all over the media provoked a visceral reaction from Gaetano. It offended him deeply. Poppy was his wife and the secrets of her body were his and not for sharing. He wanted to punch walls and tear things apart. He was ablaze with a dark, violent fury that had very little to do with the fact that another scandal around his name would once again drag the proud name of the Leonetti Bank into disrepute. In fact his whole reaction felt disturbingly personal.

'Not feigning,' Poppy framed raggedly, pushing her hands down on the table top to rise again.

'I want the truth. If you had told me about this, I would never have married you,' Gaetano fired at her without hesitation.

Poppy flopped back down into the seat because her legs refused to support her. She felt really ill and believed she must have caught the flu. He would never have married her had he known about the photo. Who would ever have thought that Gaetano, the notorious womaniser, would be that narrow-minded? And why should she care? And yet she *did* care. A lone stinging tear trickled from the corner of her eye and once again she tried to get up and leave but she couldn't catch her breath. It was as though a giant stone were compressing her lungs. In panic at that air deprivation her hands flailed up to her throat, warding off the darkness that was claiming her.

Gaetano gazed in disbelief at Poppy as she virtually slithered off the chair down onto the floor and lay there unconscious, as pale and still as a corpse. And all of a sudden the publication of nude photos of *his* wife was no longer his most overriding concern...

CHAPTER EIGHT

'No, I DON'T think that my wife has an eating disorder,' Gaetano bit out between gritted teeth in the waiting room.

'Signora Leonetti is seriously underweight, dehydrated...in generally poor physical condition,' the doctor outlined disapprovingly. 'That is why the bacterial infection has gained such a hold on her and why we are still struggling to get her temperature under control. That she contrived to get through a wedding and travel in such a state has to be a miracle.'

'A miracle...' Gaetano whispered, sick to his stomach and, for the very first time in his brilliantly successful, high-achieving life, feeling like a failure.

How else could he feel? Poppy had collapsed.

His wife was wearing an oxygen mask in the IC unit, having drugs pumped into her. All right, she hadn't told him how she was feeling but shouldn't a normal, decent human being have *noticed* that something was wrong?

Unfortunately he clearly couldn't claim to be a normal, decent human being. And his analytical mind left him in no doubt of exactly where he had gone wrong. He had been too busy admiring his bride's tiny waist to register that she was dangerously thin. He had been too busy dragging her off to bed to register that she was unwell. And when she had tried to tell him, what had he done? *Porca miseria*, he had shouted at her and accused her of feigning illness!

'May I see her now?' he asked thickly.

He stood at the foot of the bed looking at Poppy through fresh eyes, rigorously blocking the sexual allure that screwed with his brain. Ironically she had always impressed him as being so lively, energetic and opinionated that he had instinctively endowed her with a glowing health that she did not possess. Now that she was silent and lying there so still, he could see how vulnerable she really was. It was etched in the fine bones of her face, the slenderness of her arms, the exhaustion he could clearly see in the bluish shadows below her eyes.

And what else would she be but exhausted? he asked himself grimly. For months she had worked two jobs, managing the hall and working at the bar. She had been so busy looking after her mother and her brother that she had forgotten to look after herself. He suspected that she had got out of the habit then of taking regular meals and rest. And even when both food and rest had been on offer in London she had *still* chosen to work every day at that café. In truth she was as much of a workaholic in her proud and stubborn independence as he was, he acknowledged bleakly. He could only hope that he was correct in believing that she did not suffer from an underlying eating disorder.

'Your grandfather is waiting outside…' a nurse informed him.

'There was no need for you to leave your bed,' Gaetano scolded the older man. 'I only texted you so that you would know where I was.'

'How is she?' Rodolfo asked worriedly.

And Gaetano told him, withholding nothing. 'I've been a pretty lousy husband so far,' he breathed in grim conclusion, conceding the point before it could be made for him.

'You have a steep learning curve in front of you.' His grandfather sighed. 'But she's a wonderful girl and well worth the effort. And it's not where you start out that matters, Gaetano…it's where you end up.'

Rodolfo could not have been more wrong in that estimate, Gaetano reflected austerely. Where you started out mattered very much if you had previously blocked the road to journey's end. His marriage was not a marriage and the relationship was already faltering. He had put up a roadblock with the word divorce on it and used that as an excuse to behave badly. He had screwed up. He had been shockingly selfish and with Poppy of all people, Poppy who had trailed round after him and his dog, Dino, on the estate when they were both kids. And what had she been like then?

Like an irritating little kid sister. Kind, madly affectionate, his biggest fan. He exhaled heavily. He had had more compassion as a boy than he had retained as an adult and he had not lived up to Poppy's high expectations. Worse still, he had taken advantage of her despair over her family's predicament. He had forced through the terms he wanted, terms she should have denied for her own sake, terms only a complete selfish bastard would have demanded. But it was a little too late to turn that particular clock back.

Was the selfishness a Leonetti trait? His father had been the ultimate egotist and his mother had never in her life, to his knowledge, put anyone's needs before her own. Had his dysfunctional parents made him the ruthless predator that he was at heart? Or had wealth and success and boundless ambition irrevocably changed him? Gaetano asked himself grimly.

Poppy surfaced to appreciate that her head had stopped aching. She discovered that she could swallow again and that her breath was no longer trapped in her chest. She opened her eyes on the unfamiliar room, taking in the hospital bed and the drip attached to her arm before focusing on Gaetano, who was hunched in the chair in the corner.

Gaetano looked as if he had been dragged through hell and far removed from the sophisticated, exquisitely groomed image that was the norm for him. His black curls were tousled, his jaw line heavily stubbled. His jacket was missing. His shirt was open at his brown throat and his sleeves were rolled up. As she stared he lifted his head and she collided with glorious dark golden eyes.

Snatches of memory engulfed her in broken bits and pieces. She remembered the passion and the pleasure he had shown her. Then she remembered his fury about the nude photos, his refusal to credit that she was ill. But she remembered nothing after that point.

Gaetano stood up and pressed the bell on the wall. 'How are you feeling?'

'Better than I felt when I fainted...er...did I faint?'

'You passed out. Next time you feel ill, *tell me*,' he breathed with grim urgency.

Poppy grimaced. 'It was our first night together.'

'That's irrelevant. Your health comes first... *always*,' he stressed. 'I'm not a little boy. I can deal with disappointment.'

She was relieved to see that his anger had gone. A nurse came in and went through a series of checks with her.

'Why did I pass out?' Poppy asked Gaetano once the nurse had departed.

'You had an infection and it ran out of control. Your immune system was too weak to fight it off,' he shared flatly. 'From here on in you have to take better care of yourself. But first, give me an honest answer to one question…do you have an eating disorder?'

'No, of course not. I'm naturally skinny…well, I have lost weight over the last few months,' she conceded grudgingly.

'You have to eat more,' Gaetano decreed. 'No more skipping meals.'

'I didn't eat on our wedding day because I wasn't feeling well,' she protested.

'Am I so intimidating that you couldn't tell me that?' Gaetano asked, springing restively upright again to pace round the spacious room.

'Come on, Gaetano. All those guests, all that fuss. What bride would have wanted to be a party pooper?'

'You should have told me that night,' Gaetano asserted.

Poppy's lashes lowered over her strained eyes. 'You weren't in the mood to hear that I was ill.'

'*Dio mio!* It shouldn't have mattered how I felt!'

A flush drove away her pallor but she kept her gaze firmly fixed on the bed. 'We had an agreement.'

'That's over, forget about it,' Gaetano bit out in a raw undertone.

She wondered what he meant and would have questioned him but the doctor arrived and there was no opportunity. Gaetano spoke to the older man at length in Italian. Breakfast arrived on a tray and she ate with appetite, mindful of the doctor's warning that she needed to regain the weight she had lost. She was smothering a yawn when Gaetano lifted the tray away.

'Get some sleep,' he urged. 'I'm going back to the house to shower and change and bring you back some clothes. As long as you promise to eat and rest, I can take you out of here this evening.'

'I'm not an invalid...' Uneasy with his forbidding attitude, Poppy fiddled with her wedding ring, turning it round and round on her finger. 'What's happened about the photos you mentioned?'

Gaetano froze and then he reached for the jacket on the chair and withdrew a folded piece of paper. 'It was a hoax…'

The newspaper cutting depicted a reproduction of a calendar shot headed Miss July. In it Poppy was reclining on a chaise longue with her bare shoulders and long legs on display while a giant floral arrangement was sited to block any more intimate view of her body.

'I kept my knickers on,' she told him ruefully. 'But I had to take my bra off because the straps showed. I was a student nurse on the ladies' football team. We did the charity calendar to raise funds for the children's hospice. There was nothing the slightest bit raunchy about the shots. It was all good, clean fun…'

Dark colour now rode along Gaetano's cheekbones. 'I know and I accept that. I'm sorry I shouted at you. When Rodolfo showed me that photo in the newspaper I felt like an idiot.'

'No, you're not an idiot.' Just very *very* possessive in a way Poppy had not expected him to be.

My wife, he had growled, outraged by the prospect of anyone else seeing her naked.

'You have an old-fashioned streak that I never would have guessed you had,' Poppy remarked tentatively.

'What is mine is mine and you are mine,' Gaetano informed her in a gut reaction that took control of him before he could even think about what he was saying.

That gut reaction utterly unnerved him. What the hell was wrong with him? *Mine?* Since when? Only weeks earlier he would have leapt on the excuse of inappropriate nude photos to break off their supposed engagement. He had not intended to stay engaged to Poppy for very long at all, had actually been depending on her to do or say something dreadful to give him a good reason to reclaim his freedom. How had he travelled from that frame of mind to his current one? All of a sudden she felt like his wife, his *real* wife. Why was that? Sex had never meant that much to Gaetano and had certainly never opened any doors to deeper connections. But he had wanted Poppy as he had never wanted any woman before and that hunger had triumphed.

Poppy went pink. 'Not really...'

'For as long as you wear that ring you're mine,' Gaetano qualified.

Poppy hadn't needed that reminder of her true status, hadn't sought that more detailed interpretation. Her heart sank and she closed her eyes to shut out his lean, darkly handsome features. It was no good because she still saw his beautiful face in her mind's eye.

'Lie down, relax,' Gaetano urged. 'You're exhausted. I'll be back later.'

You're mine. But she wasn't. She was a fake bride and a temporary wife. Casual sex didn't grant her any status. Suppressing a groan, she shut down her brain on her teeming thoughts and fell asleep.

Late that afternoon, she left the hospital in a wheelchair in spite of her protests. In truth she still felt weak and woozy. Gaetano lifted her out of the chair and stowed her carefully in the passenger seat before joining her.

She was wearing the faded denim sundress Dolores had packed for her.

'I need to organise new clothes for you,' Gaetano told her.

'No, you don't. When this finishes we go our separate ways and I won't have any use for fancy threads.'

'But *this* isn't going to finish any time soon,' Gaetano pointed out softly.

Poppy studied his bold bronzed profile. So far they had enjoyed the honeymoon from hell but he was bearing up well to the challenge. His caring, compassionate husband act was off-the-charts good but she guessed that was purely for Rodolfo's benefit. They were supposed to be in love, after all, and a loving husband would be upset when his bride fell ill on their wedding day. Lush black lashes curled up as he turned his head to look at her, blue-black hair gleaming in the bright light, spectacular golden eyes wary.

'What's wrong?' he prompted.

'I should compliment you. You can fake nice to the manner born,' she quipped.

His wide sensual mouth compressed. For once there was no witty comeback. 'Dolores is planning to fatten you up on pasta. I also mentioned that you're passionate about chocolate.'

Chocolate and Gaetano, she corrected inwardly.

She collided with his eyes and hurriedly looked away, struggling not to revel in the sound of his dark, deep, accented drawl and the high she got from the sheer charisma of his smile. Awareness shimmied through her like an electrical storm. Something low in her tummy had turned molten and liquid while her breasts were swelling inside her bra. He had taught her to want him, she thought bitterly, and now the wanting wouldn't conveniently go away. That hunger was like a slow burn building inside her.

When they returned to La Fattoria, Gaetano insisted that she went straight to bed and dined there. He ignored her declaration that she was feeling well enough to come downstairs and urged her to follow medical advice and rest. A large collection of books and DVDs were delivered mid-evening for her entertainment and although Poppy was tired she deliberately stayed awake waiting for Gaetano to come to bed. She drifted off around one in the morning and wakened to see Gaetano switching out the light and walking back to the door.

'Where are you going?' she mumbled.

'I'm sleeping next door,' he said wryly.

'That's not necessary.' Poppy had to fight to keep the hurt note out of her voice. She had been looking forward to Gaetano putting his arms around her again and she was disappointed that it wasn't going to happen.

'I'm a restless sleeper. I don't want to disturb you,' Gaetano countered smoothly.

Poppy's heart sank as if he had kicked it. Maybe if sex wasn't on the menu, Gaetano preferred to sleep alone. And why would she argue about that? It was possible that Gaetano had already had all he really wanted from her. She had heard about men who lost sexual interest once the novelty was gone. One night might have been enough for him. Was he that kind of lover? And if he was, what did it matter to her? It wasn't as if she were about to embarrass herself and chase after him, was it? Why would she do that when their eventual separation and divorce were already set in stone?

So, it didn't make sense that after he had gone she curled up in the big bed feeling lonely and needy and rejected. Why on earth was she bothered?

'You shouldn't be down here keeping an old man company,' Rodolfo reproved as Poppy poured his coffee and her own. 'No cake?'

'Cinzia's putting it on a fancy plate to bring it out. You're getting spoiled,' Poppy told him fondly, perching on the low wall of the terrace.

His bright dark eyes twinkled. 'Nothing wrong

with being spoiled. You spoil me with your cakes but Gaetano's supposed to be spoiling you.'

Poppy's luminous green eyes shadowed. 'He does but I've let him off the honeymoon trail for a few hours to work. It keeps him happy...'

'You look well,' Gaetano's grandfather said approvingly. 'On your wedding day you looked as though a strong breeze would blow you over, now you look...'

'Fatter?' Poppy laughed. 'You can say it. I'd got too thin and I look better carrying a little more weight. Dolores has been feeding me up like a Christmas turkey.'

Hands banded round her raised knees, Poppy gazed out over the valley, scanning the marching rows of bright green vines. The property referred to as the guest house was a substantial building surrounded by trees and it had a spectacular view. It had always been Rodolfo's favourite spot and when he had tired of his late son's constant parties at the main house he had built his own bolt-hole.

Cinzia, who looked after the guest house and its elderly occupant, brought out the lemon drizzle cake that Poppy had baked.

Poppy and Gaetano had been in Tuscany for a whole month, days fleeing past at a speed she could barely register. As soon as she had regained her strength, Gaetano had begun taking her out sightseeing. Her brain was crammed to bursting point by magnificent artworks and architectural wonders. But the memories that lingered were of a rather more personal variety.

Her delicate gold earrings were a gift from Gaetano, purchased from one of the spectacular goldsmiths on the Ponte Vecchio in Florence. In Pisa they had strolled through the magical streets to dine after the daily visitors had left and he had told her that in bright light her red hair reminded him of a gorgeous sunset. In Lucca they had walked the city walls in the leafy shade of the overhanging trees and Gaetano had briefly held her hand to steady her. In Siena she had proved Gaetano wrong when he'd told her that climbing more than four hundred steps to the top of the Torre del Mangia would be too much for her and he had laughed and given her that special heart-stopping smile that somehow always rocked her world. And in the Grotta del Vento he had whipped off his jacket and wrapped it round her when he'd seen her shiver in the coolness of the underground cave system.

Personal memories but not the romantic memories of a newly married couple, Poppy conceded unhappily. There was no sex. There had been no sex since she had taken ill and he refused to take hints. And she refused to count as romantic all the many evenings they had talked long and late at the farmhouse after a beautiful leisurely meal because every evening had ended with them occupying separate beds.

Indeed, Gaetano only got close to her in his grandfather's presence, clearly as part of his effort to keep up the pretence that they were a normal couple, and then he would close his arms round her, kiss her shoulder or her cheek, act as if he were a touchy-feely loving male even though he wasn't. His determined detachment often made Poppy want to scream and slap him into a normal reaction. What had happened to the sex-hungry male who couldn't keep his hands off her?

And while Poppy was lying awake irritating herself by wondering how to tempt Gaetano without being too obvious about it and scolding herself for being so defensive, another bigger worry slowly began to percolate in the back of her mind. At first she had told herself off for being foolish. After all, they had only had sex once and she had conscientiously taken the contraceptive pill from the first day it was prescribed to her. When her period was late she had believed that her illness or even the change of diet or stress could have messed up her menstrual cycle. As the days trickled past her subdued sense of panic had steadily mounted and she was very glad that she was visiting the doctor the following day for an official review following her release from hos-

pital a month earlier. She would ask for a pregnancy test then just to be on the safe side. And of
course she would soon realise that she had been
foolishly worrying over nothing. There was no
way she could possibly be pregnant.

Leaving Rodolfo snoozing in the shade, Poppy
clicked her fingers to bring Muffin gambolling
to her side as she strolled back to the main house.

Muffin had made a full recovery from his inju-
ries and had been inseparable from Poppy from
the day Gaetano had brought him back from the
vet's and settled the little terrier in his wife's
lap. The dog ran ahead as Poppy walked below
the trees enjoying the cool shade rather than the
heat of late afternoon. She smiled at the colourful glimpses of poppy-and-sunflower-studded
fields visible through the gaps between the trees.

Since the wedding she had talked to her mother
and brother every week on the phone. Damien
was happy in his new job while her mother had
renewed contact with Poppy's aunt, Jess, who had
stopped seeing her sister when she became an al-

coholic. Now there was talk of Poppy's mother going to live with her sister in Manchester after she was released.

That idea left Poppy feeling oddly abandoned and she told herself off for her selfishness because it was not as if she herself would be in a position to set up home with her mother any time soon. No, Poppy was very conscious that she had a long, hard haul ahead of her faking being happily married to Gaetano for at least a couple of years. And if she was miserable, well, she accepted that that was her own fault as well. If her emotions made her miserable it was because she had failed to control them. Her craving for Gaetano's attention had been the first warning sign, missing him in bed after only one night the second. From that point on the warning signs had simply multiplied into a terrifying avalanche.

If Gaetano held her hand, she felt light-headed. If he touched her she lit up inside like a firework. If he smiled her heart soared. Her adolescent crush had grown into something much more dangerous, something she couldn't control and that occasionally overwhelmed her. She had fallen madly, insanely in love with the husband who wasn't a husband. It wasn't fair that Gaetano should be so beautiful that she found intense pleasure in simply looking at him. It was even less fair that he was such entertaining company and had wonderful manners. Nor did it help that he took great pains to ensure that she ate well and rested often, revealing a caring side she had only previously seen in play around his grandfather. It was all a cheat, she kept on telling herself. It was a cheat because he wasn't available to her in any way even though she loved him.

She *loved* Gaetano. She was ashamed of that truth when he had warned her not to make that mistake long before he'd even married her. How had she turned out so predictable? It was not as if she believed in the pot of gold at the end of the rainbow. She was not a dreamer now that she had grown up. She knew that no happy ending awaited her and she would cope as long as she contrived to keep her emotional attachment to herself because she would die a thousand deaths before she allowed Gaetano to even suspect how she felt. He hadn't asked for love from her and he didn't want her love. No way was he getting her love for free so that he could pity her.

A fancy sports car that didn't belong to Gaetano's collection was parked outside La Fattoria. Poppy smoothed down her exotic black and red sundress, one of the designer garments Gaetano had purchased for her weeks ago. It was cutting-edge style and edgy enough to feel comfortable to her, so she had acquiesced to the new wardrobe, mortified by the suspicion that for her to insist on continuing to wear cheap clothing would embarrass Gaetano. No, he might deserve a kick for seducing her with unforgettable enthusiasm and then stopping that intimacy in its tracks, but she still cringed at the idea of embarrassing him in public.

Gaetano saw his wife from the front window, her show-stopping long legs silhouetted beneath the thin fabric of her dress. It was see-through, and it killed him to see her legs and recall that one indescribably hot night when he had slid between them. Feeling his trousers tighten, he gritted his teeth. The sooner he was out of their marriage and free again, the more normal he would feel.

In truth nothing had felt normal since their wedding. Being around Poppy without being able to touch her was driving him insane. He had a high sex drive and he had never tried to suppress it before. But for the first time in his life with a woman he was trying to do the right thing and it was hurting like a bitch. Poppy deserved more than he had to give. But inexplicably Poppy had got under his skin and since he had laid eyes on her no other woman had attracted him. Although he'd satisfied himself sexually with her, he still desired her, which was a first for him. The thrill of the chase had gone, but the hunger lingered, ever present, ever powerful. There was something about her that affected him differently from other women. She didn't irritate him, she didn't make demands, she didn't care about his money. In the strangest of ways she reminded him of his grandmother, who had been as at home with staff as she was with visitors. Poppy's easy charm was spread wide and he no longer marvelled that Rodolfo idolised her and the household staff couldn't do enough for her. Even that ugly little dog was her devoted slave.

'Sorry...I needed to freshen up,' Serena announced as she walked back into the drawing room. 'I got blown to bits. I forgot to tie my hair back before I drove over.'

Gaetano studied the smooth golden veil of Serena's hair. He had never seen her with a hair out of place. Poppy's hair got madly tangled, but she didn't care. It had been wild that night in bed, he recalled, fighting off arousal as he pictured that vibrant mane tumbled across the pillows, her lovely face flushed and full of satisfaction, satisfaction *he* had given her.

Poppy entered and froze at the sight of Serena. 'Sorry, I didn't realise you had company.'

'Oh, I'm not company. I'm one of Gaetano's oldest friends,' Serena reminded her. 'How are you, Poppy? I would have called in sooner, but it is your honeymoon, after all.'

'Are you staying round here?'

'Didn't Gaetano tell you that my parents have had a house near here for years and years? We first met at one of his parents' parties when we were teenagers,' Serena told her with a golden-girl smile of fond familiarity aimed at Gaetano.

Serena was the wicked witch in the disguise of a beautiful princess, Poppy decided bleakly. Serena knew exactly where to plunge the knife and twist it in another's woman's flesh. She loved to boast of how well, how intimately and how long she had known Gaetano. 'Fancy that,' she said non-committally.

'I'm actually here to beg for a favour,' Serena confided cutely. 'I met Rodolfo in the village last week and he told me that Gaetano was flying to Paris for a conference tomorrow. May I come too? As you know I'm looking for a new job and I could use the introductions you'd give me.'

'Of course. I'll pick you up on the way to the airport,' Gaetano suggested calmly.

Hell no, Poppy thought, watching Serena look at Gaetano with a teasing girly smile and a shake of her golden head that sent the silken strands tossing round her perfect face. Her teeth ground together.

'Are you coming too?' Serena asked Poppy.

But Poppy could see that somehow Serena had already established that Gaetano would be travelling to Paris alone. 'No, I'm afraid I have an appointment to keep,' Poppy admitted.

'I wish you'd agreed to reschedule that. I wanted to accompany you,' Gaetano reminded her with detectable exasperation.

Poppy wrinkled her nose. 'It's only a check-up.'

And she didn't want him attending the doctor's surgery with her because she didn't want him present for the discussion of the pregnancy possibility.

'I could cancel and come to Paris with you,' she heard herself offer abruptly, because she really didn't want Serena getting the chance to be alone with Gaetano.

'You need to keep that appointment,' Gaetano countered levelly. 'In any case, I'll be back by evening.'

'I'll look after him,' Serena assured her smugly and Poppy wondered unhappily if the other woman somehow sensed that Gaetano's marriage was not quite normal. Or was it simply that the beautiful blonde could not imagine a male as well educated and sophisticated as Gaetano marrying an ordinary woman without there being some hidden agenda?

She had paled at Serena's self-satisfaction. Gaetano had not been with a woman in a month. Naturally Poppy didn't want him on board his private jet with a man-eater like Serena. Serena was already putting out willing and welcome signals as bright as traffic lights. But what could Poppy possibly say to Gaetano to inhibit him in

such a marriage as theirs? He didn't belong to
her. She didn't own him.

There were other ways of holding onto a man's
attention though, she reasoned abstractedly. There
was using sex as a weapon, exactly the sort of
manipulative behaviour she had looked down on
before she fell in love with Gaetano. Now, all of
a sudden confronted by Serena studying Gaetano
as though he were one of the seven wonders of the
world, Poppy's stance on the moral high ground
felt foolish and dangerous. Pride wouldn't keep
her warm at night if Gaetano succumbed to
Serena's advances and embarked on an affair with
her. An affair that Poppy suspected would soon
be followed by divorce and remarriage because
she didn't believe that Serena would accept being
hidden in the background or that Gaetano would
resist the chance to acquire a woman who would
make a much more suitable wife.

Gaetano released his breath in a slow hiss when
Poppy joined him for dinner in a black halter-

necked dress that outlined her lithe, slender figure. His intense dark gaze rested briefly on the taut little buds of her breasts that were clearly defined by the thin fabric and he compressed his lips round his wine glass. Look, *don't* touch, he told himself grimly.

'I've been wondering,' he remarked. 'What made you choose nursing?'

Surprised by the topic, Poppy lifted and dropped her bare shoulders. 'I like caring for people. Being needed makes me feel useful.'

'Your family certainly needed you,' Gaetano said drily.

The main course was served. After eating in silence for a few minutes Poppy said, 'I'm thinking of doing something other than nursing when the time comes.'

'Such as?' Gaetano prompted impatiently.

'Gardening,' she admitted in a defensive tone.

'Gardening?' Gaetano repeated with incredulity.

'I always discounted my interest in growing

things because I come from several generations of gardeners. But I suppose it's in my blood,' Poppy opined wryly. 'Of course if I'd ever mentioned it I would have found myself working for your family and I didn't want that.'

'I've never understood why not. We're good employers.'

'Yes, but working on the estate means real old-fashioned service.'

'And what is bartending but service?' Gaetano watched her turn to lift her water glass and his attention dropped to the firm, full, pouting curve of her breast revealed by her dress. He shifted tensely in his seat.

'There's not that same sense of inequality between employer and employee that there is on the estate. I can't explain it but I've never accepted that you are superior to me simply because you were born into wealth and privilege.'

'Have I ever made you feel that way?'

Poppy pushed away her plate and stood up. 'You can't help it. Your parents raised you like that.'

'Where are you going?'

'For a walk—it's a beautiful evening. I'll have space for dessert by the time I come back,' she told Sean, who was hovering to remove their plates.

'I'll come too.' Gaetano sprang upright.

Poppy was as restless as a cat on hot bricks, which was hardly surprising when she had set herself the objective of somehow seducing Gaetano before his flight to Paris. Sadly discussing her career aspirations and the class system wouldn't get her any closer to him and she wasn't very deft at flirting. If all else failed, she thought ruefully, she would simply slip into bed with him and pray that his libido cracked his detachment.

'That's a daring dress,' Gaetano observed. 'The split in the skirt shows me your thighs at every step and I can see the curve and shape of your breasts. Don't wear it anywhere more public...'

Poppy was relieved that he had actually noticed the provocative outfit because it meant that she wasn't yet fading into the wallpaper as far as he was concerned. Her high heels crunched through the gravel. A finger danced up her exposed spine like a flame licking at her bare skin and she shivered, snatching in a breath as he flicked the knot at the nape of her neck. 'If I pulled that loose...'

'The whole thing would probably fall off,' she completed.

Gaetano groaned out loud. 'Don't tempt me.'

'I didn't think you could be tempted any more.'

'Temptation runs on a continuous loop around you.'

Poppy glanced at him with disbelieving eyes. 'Then why have you been keeping your distance?'

'It should've been that way from the start, *bellezza mia*. I was a selfish bastard to insist on sex.'

'So, tell me something new,' Poppy invited.

After a moment of telling silence, Gaetano's stunning dark golden gaze locked to her flushed face in near wonderment at that response before he burst out laughing. 'Well, that's telling me…'

'If you wanted lies you married the wrong girl.'

'Obviously,' Gaetano conceded, lounging back against an aged stone pedestal table at the viewpoint where the land fell away to reveal the panoramic landscape beyond the garden. Poppy gazed out at the beautiful countryside, her hair glowing like a live flame against her ivory skin as the sun went down.

'I'm not being fair to you,' Poppy muttered with sudden awkwardness. 'I wanted sex too!'

'Maybe when we were actually having it but not before,' Gaetano qualified.

'Oh, for goodness' sake, Gaetano…I couldn't *wait* to rip your clothes off!' Poppy flung back at him in exasperation. 'I didn't stay a virgin until this age by not knowing what I wanted. I'm not some easily led little rag doll. Stop talking as if you took advantage of a naïve kid!'

'But I *did* take advantage of you.' Gaetano reached out to grip both her hands in emphasis and prevent her from her constant pacing back and forth in front of him. 'You were a virgin and I'm a natural predator. What I want I take. And I very much wanted you.'

Poppy took a step closer to his lean, powerful body. 'How much is "very much"?'

He brought her hands down lightly to the revealing bulge at his groin. Her fingertips fluttered appreciatively over the hard jut of his erection and he jerked in surprise at that intimate caress. His golden eyes smouldering with erotic heat, he pulled her up against him and crushed her ripe pink mouth beneath his, his tongue darting and delving deep to send tiny shudders of shocking arousal coursing through her lower body. Liquid heat pooled between her thighs.

'You're a tease,' Gaetano told her darkly.

'No, I'm a sure thing,' Poppy contradicted, helpless in the grip of the need throbbing and pulsing through her trembling length.

She felt the sudden give at her neck as he tugged loose the tie of her dress. As the bodice dropped to her waist his hands closed to her hips and he lifted her up onto the stone table before reaching below the skirt to close his hands into the waistband of her lace knickers and yank them down.

'Out here?' she whispered, shaken by the concept as he dug her discarded underwear into his pocket with single-minded efficiency.

'Out here because I couldn't make it back indoors…and I believe I can promise you a very active night,' he husked, bending her backwards to capture a rosy nipple between his lips and lash it with his tongue while his fingers stroked and teased the delicate pink folds at her core.

'I want you,' she framed jaggedly, her breath strangled in her throat by a responsive gasp as his thumb rubbed over her and then a long finger tested her readiness.

He slid a single digit into her lush opening and her body jackknifed, spine arching, hips lifting off the cold stone surface. And the coldness below her only added to the intense heat punching through her quivering body, steamrollering over her inhibitions and heightening every sensation to an unbearable level.

'So wet, so tight,' Gaetano growled, yanking down his zip with a lack of cool that even in the state he was in astounded him. On some level the hunger was so all-consuming that he honestly thought he might die of overexcitement if he didn't get inside her.

His mouth roved between the straining mounds of her perfect breasts, tugging at the swollen buds, arrowing lower, letting her feel the long, slow glide of his tongue while he pulled her to the edge of the table to position her.

He plunged in and drove the breath from her body with the intensity of his entrance. She whimpered as he stretched her, her body clenching round him like a hot velvet glove.

'*So* good,' Gaetano ground out between gritted teeth as he pulled back and slammed back into her with delicious force.

Poppy couldn't think, she could only feel and she was riding a torrent of excitement she couldn't control, her entire being pitched to crave the peak of his every powerful thrust. The heat and the hunger and the pleasure all melded together into one glorious, overwhelming rush of sexual ecstasy. Her climax claimed her in an explosive surge of intense sensation and her teeth bit into his shoulder as the exquisite convulsions shook her violently in his arms.

In the aftermath she was as limp as a floppy doll. He fed her feet back into her underwear, retied her dress and lifted her down to the ground again where she swayed, utterly undone by the sheer primal wildness of their joining.

'Did I hurt you?'

'No, you blew me away,' she whispered truthfully.

'You bring out the animal in me, *delizia mia*,' he admitted raggedly, pressing his sensual mouth to the top of her down-bent head in what felt like a silent apology.

'And I like it,' Poppy admitted shakily. 'I like it very much.'

'What the hell have we been playing at, then, for the last few weeks?' he demanded.

Poppy shot him a teasing glance. 'You were depriving me of sex. Why, I have no idea.'

But Gaetano was in not in the mood to talk. He was already painfully aware of the lack of logic in his recent behaviour. He couldn't answer his own questions, never mind explain or defend his decisions to her. He had honestly believed that for once he was doing the honourable thing and that she would appreciate his restraint. Evidently he had got that badly wrong. She was accusing him of depriving her. *Diavelos*...no doubt it was sexist but he was the one who had felt most deprived. And being deprived of the joy of her body had eased his conscience.

His brooding silence nagged at Poppy's nerves. Perhaps even though he enjoyed the physical release of her body he had preferred the distance provided by their lack of intimacy. Maybe he was worried she was getting too attached. Maybe she wasn't as good an actress as she liked to believe.

'It was just sex, you know,' she mumbled as lightly as she could. 'It doesn't have to mean anything.'

'I know,' Gaetano fielded drily while also knowing that he could never, ever have imagined having a wife who would admit that she had just used him for sex.

It felt wrong to him and downright offensive but he was willing to admit that getting married to Poppy and living with her while struggling to stay out of her bed had played merry hell with his values. One hint of encouragement from her and he had shelved honour without a backward glance. In fact he'd been a pushover, he conceded grimly. He craved her like a drug. He was already thinking of early nights, dawn takeovers and afternoon siestas, hopefully the kinkier, the better, because his bride was still on a wonderful learning curve. Did it really matter if she only wanted him for sex?

Why complicate something simple? She was right. It was just sex, not something he had ever felt the need to agonise over or attach labels to. *Maledizione!* What was she doing to his brain? Why was he dwelling on something so basic?

CHAPTER NINE

'I BELIEVE THE medication you received in hospital may have disrupted your birth control. Of course, no contraceptive pill is foolproof either. It's an interesting conundrum,' Mr Abramo remarked as if the development were purely one of academic interest. 'Fortunately you're in much better health than you were a month ago…absolutely blooming, in fact!'

Poppy's smile felt stiff because she was still in shock. She was pregnant, one hundred per cent with no room for error pregnant and Gaetano was likely to go into even greater shock over that reality. One night, one bout of passion, one baby. Obviously, Gaetano would feel that he had been very unlucky. What were the odds of such a development? What would he want to do? How would he react? She was already praying that he would not hope that she might be willing to consider a termination.

While it was true that she hadn't planned on a baby, she still wanted the child that was now on its way. Her baby and Gaetano's, a little piece of Leonetti heritage that even Gaetano couldn't take off her again, divorce or otherwise. A little boy, a little girl, Poppy wasn't fussy about the gender. Indeed she was getting excited about the prospect of motherhood and feeling guilty about the fact. How could she dare to look forward happily to an event that would probably seriously depress and infuriate Gaetano, who preferred to plan everything and liked to believe that he could control everybody and everything in his life? The baby would be a wildly out-of-control event. And Gaetano had been frank from the outset that he did not want to risk a conception when they were planning to part. Having foreseen that scenario, he had set out to prevent that situation arising.

Before her conscience could claim her and stifle her natural impulses, Poppy paid a visit to a very exclusive baby shop in Florence where without the smallest encouragement she purchased an incredibly expensive shawl and a tiny pair of exquisite white lace bootees. When she emerged again, clutching a cute beribboned bag, she saw her pair of bodyguards exchanging knowing looks and, scolding herself for her mindless compulsion, made a hurried comment about needing wrapping paper for her gift.

When she returned to La Fattoria for lunch, Gaetano was still in Paris. But he might well have fallen asleep during the flight there, Poppy thought with a wicked little smile. Quite deliberately she had exhausted him. A sexually satiated tired male was unlikely to be tempted by the offer of sex on the side. She had kept him up half the night and had awakened him at dawn in a manner that he had sworn was the ultimate male fantasy. His response had been incredibly enthusiastic. But then Gaetano had remarkable stamina, she reflected sunnily. She ached all over. She ached in places she hadn't known she could ache but it had all been in a good cause. Surely Serena could no longer be considered a threat?

Given the smallest excuse, Gaetano would have abandoned Serena at the airport. Her incessant flirtatiousness had begun to irritate him during the flight back. Raunchy jokes about bankers and the mile-high club had fallen on stony ground. Gaetano had partied on board when he'd acquired his first private jet but those irresponsible days were far behind him now that he was in the act of becoming the new CEO of the Leonetti Bank. He was quietly satisfied by the attainment of that long-held ambition but he had spent far more time choosing a gift for Poppy during a break between meetings than he had spent considering his lofty rise in status. Ironically now that he had that status it meant less than he had expected to him. His focus in life had definitely shifted in a different direction.

Poppy got sleepy in the late afternoon and went for a nap. She lay on the bed wondering about how best to share her news with Gaetano and tears prickled her eyes because she feared his reaction. He wasn't likely to be happy about her pregnancy and she had to accept that. It would drive them apart, not keep them together. Fate had thrown them something that couldn't be easily worked around.

Gaetano was strangely disappointed when Poppy didn't greet him downstairs as Muffin did. Muffin hurled himself cheerfully at Gaetano's legs, refused to sit when told and barked like mad. Muffin didn't discriminate. Everyone who came through the front door received the same boisterous, undisciplined welcome. Dolores informed Gaetano that Poppy had gone up to lie down and concern quickened the long strides with which he mounted the stairs. Suddenly Gaetano was worrying about what the doctor might have told his wife about her health because taking forty winks in the evening was more Rodolfo's style.

As Gaetano entered the bedroom, Poppy,

roused by Muffin's barks, pushed herself up on her elbows and smiled, tousled red hair falling round her sleep-flushed face.

'I exhausted you last night,' Gaetano assumed with a wolfish grin of all-male satisfaction as he stood at the foot of the bed. 'I wondered what you were doing in bed and started worrying about what Mr Abramo might have said but that was before I remembered that you had another very good reason to need some extra rest.'

'It's the heat. It makes me feel drowsy.' Butterflies danced to a jungle beat in her tummy while she studied him.

In his beautifully tailored designer suit, Gaetano was a vision of masculine elegance and sex appeal. He was gorgeous with dark stubble outlining his strong jaw line and those intense dark eyes below his extraordinary lashes. Her breasts tingled and heat simmered low in her pelvis.

'It's weird because I've only been away a few hours...but I missed you,' Gaetano confided in a constrained undertone. 'What did Mr Abramo have to say?'

Poppy tensed and swung her legs off the side of the bed so that she was half turned away from him. 'He had some news for me after the tests,' she told him tautly.

'What sort of news?' Gaetano prompted, shedding his jacket and jerking loose his tie while wondering if she would consider him excessively demanding and greedy if he joined her on the bed.

'Unexpected news,' Poppy qualified tightly. 'You're going to be surprised.'

'So, go ahead and surprise me,' Gaetano urged, unsettled by her uncharacteristic reluctance to meet his eyes and shelving the sexual trail to force his brain to focus.

'I'm pregnant.' She framed the words curtly, refusing to sound apologetic or nervous, putting it out there exactly like the fact of life it was.

'How could you possibly be pregnant?' Gaetano shot at her with an incredulous frown. 'If it had only just happened, it would be too soon to know and the one and only other time…it isn't possible…'

'It *is* possible. I fell ill that same day and I missed taking my pill. Mr Abramo also believes the drugs I was given could have interfered with my birth control,' she told him flatly.

'You got pregnant on our wedding night?' Gaetano queried in astonishment. 'From *one* time? What are you? The fertility queen?'

'You didn't use a condom,' she reminded him.

'There shouldn't have been a risk.'

'If you're having sex there's always a risk,' she pointed out ruefully. 'The odds weren't good that night because I ended up in hospital. In any other circumstances we'd probably have got away with it.'

'Pregnant,' Gaetano repeated, expelling his breath on a long slow hiss as he paced over to the windows, the taut muscles in his lean behind and long, powerful legs braced rigid with tension. 'You're pregnant.'

Although there was little expression in his dark, deep drawl Poppy took strength from his lack of anger and his ability to joke. Gaetano was dealing with it, *wasn't he*? He was good in a crisis, very cool-headed and logical and what they had right now was undeniably a *huge* crisis. A baby nobody had counted on was on the way, a baby she would nonetheless love and protect to the best of her ability.

Gaetano was still feeling light-headed with shock. A baby! He was going to be a father? *Dio mio*...he was in no way prepared to be a parent. Having a child was a massive responsibility. It had proved a challenge too much for his own parents and even Rodolfo had struggled with the test of raising Gaetano's good-for-nothing father. How the hell would he manage? What did he have to offer a child?

'Gaetano?' Poppy probed in the tense silence.

He swung round and raked long brown fingers through his cropped black hair in a gesture of frustration. 'A baby… I can't believe it. That's some curve ball to be thrown.'

'Yes,' Poppy agreed stiffly. 'For both of us.'

'In fact it's a nightmare,' Gaetano framed, shocking her with that assessment, which was so much more pessimistic than her own.

Poppy stiffened but fought not to take that comment too personally. 'Not much I can do to change your outlook if that's how you feel.'

'I don't like the unexpected, the spontaneous,' he admitted grimly. 'A baby will turn our lives upside down.'

'But there's a positive side as well as a negative side,' Poppy murmured.

'Is there?' Gaetano traded in stark disagreement. 'We had a divorce planned.'

Poppy lost colour and screened her eyes. A *nightmare*? That had been a body blow but that his second comment on their situation should refer to their divorce was even tougher. But what had she expected from him? A bottle of champagne and whoops of satisfaction? It could have been a lot worse, she told herself urgently. Gaetano could have lost his temper. He could have tried to imply that the pregnancy was somehow more her fault than his. But then possibly he hadn't reached that stage yet. After all, he was still pretty much stunned, studying her with brilliant dark eyes that had an unusually unfocused quality. *We had a divorce planned.* He had gone straight for the jugular.

'But, obviously I couldn't possibly leave you to raise my child alone,' Gaetano completed without skipping a beat. 'Looks like we're staying together, *bella mia.*'

Poppy stiffened at his bleak intonation. 'So, you're suggesting that we should forget about getting a divorce now?'

'What else would I suggest?' Gaetano asked very drily. 'You're carrying the next generation of the Leonetti dynasty. Nobody expects you to do that alone, least of all me. Even though I had two parents they did a fairly rubbish job of raising me. To thrive, our child will need both of us and a stable home to grow up in.'

'But it's not what we planned,' Poppy reminded him while anger simmered like a pot bubbling on the hob beneath her careful surface show of calm.

There was nothing to be gained from losing her temper, she told herself fiercely, but his practical approach was downright insulting. Yes, she agreed that ideally a child should have both parents and a steady home but at what cost? If the parents themselves made sacrifices that resulted in unhappiness how could that be good for anyone? Poppy did not want an unwilling husband and reluctant father by her side. That was not a cross she was prepared to bear for years knowing that it wouldn't benefit anyone. If that was the best Gaetano had to offer, he could keep it and the wedding ring, she thought painfully. She wanted more, she *needed* more than a man who would only keep her as a wife because she had fallen pregnant.

'We couldn't possibly make a bigger mess of

our marriage than my parents did,' he pointed out wryly. 'We can only try our best.'

'As a goal, that just depresses me, Gaetano,' Poppy admitted.

'How? We'll continue on as we are now but at least we won't be living a lie for Rodolfo's benefit any longer.'

'No, *you* won't need to live a lie any longer,' Poppy agreed tightly as she walked towards the door.

'Where are you going?'

Powered by a furious mix of anger and pain, Poppy ignored the question and stalked up the stairs to the next floor where the luggage was stored. From the room used for that purpose she grabbed up two cases.

From his stance on the landing, Gaetano stared at her in bewilderment. 'What on earth are you doing?'

'Your nightmare is leaving you!' Poppy bit out squarely.

'I did not call you a nightmare,' Gaetano argued vehemently.

'No, you called the baby I'm having a nightmare, which was worse,' Poppy countered fiercely. 'This baby may be unplanned and a big unexpected surprise but I love it already!'

'*Dio mio*, Poppy!' Gaetano exclaimed as she yanked garments out of the built-in closets in the dressing room, hangers falling in all directions. 'Will you please calm down?'

'Why would I calm down? I'm pregnant and my husband thinks it's a nightmare!'

'I didn't mean it that way.'

'And you seem to believe that I have no choice but to stay married to you. Well, here's some news for you, Gaetano…I can have a baby and manage perfectly well without you!' Poppy slung at him from between gritted teeth. 'I don't *need* you. I deserve more. I don't intend to stay married to a guy who's only with me because he thinks it's his duty!'

'That's not what I said.'

'That's exactly what you said!' Poppy slammed a case down on the bed and wrenched it open. 'Well, this particular nightmare of yours is taking herself off. There's got to be better options than you waiting for me.'

Standing very still, Gaetano lost colour and watched her intently. 'There probably is. But I want very badly for you to stay.'

'No, you don't, not really,' Poppy reasoned thinly. 'You think our baby would be the icing on the cake for Rodolfo but you don't want to be married and you don't want to be a father.'

'I *do* want to be married to you.' Gaetano flung back his shoulders and studied her with strained dark eyes. 'And I know that I can learn how to be a good father. I meant that the situation of being unprepared for a child was a nightmare. I'm not good with surprises but I can roll fast with the punches that come my way. And believe me, watching you pack to leave me *is* a hell of a punch.'

The firm resolution in that response surprised

her. She paused to roughly fold up a dress before thrusting it into the case, sending an unimpressed glance at his lean, darkly handsome face. She wasn't listening to him, she told herself urgently. She had made her decision. It was better for her to leave him with her head held high than to consider giving him another chance...wasn't it?

'Is it? Are you really capable of changing your outlook to that extent? Accepting being married without feeling that you're somehow doing me a favour and settling for second best?' she queried with scorn. 'Accepting our child as the gift that a child is?'

'I know that I was difficult when I married you.' Gaetano compressed his lips on that startling admission. 'I'm not easy-going but I am adaptable and I do learn from my mistakes. *Dio mio, bella mia*...my attitude to you has changed most of all.'

'How?' Poppy prompted, needing him to face up to the major decision he was trying to make for both of them. She didn't want Gaetano deciding that they should stay married and then changing his mind again because he felt trapped by the restrictions. She had to know and understand exactly what he was thinking and feeling and expecting. How else could she make a decision?

His wide sensual mouth twisted. 'I don't want to discuss that.'

'Why not?'

'Because sometimes silence is golden and honesty can be the wrong way to go,' he framed grudgingly. 'And knowing my luck, I'll say the wrong thing again.'

'But you should be able to tell me anything. We shouldn't *have* secrets between us. How has your attitude to me changed?' Poppy persisted, curiosity and obstinacy combining to push her on.

Gaetano glanced heavenward for a brief moment and then drew in a ragged breath. 'I asked you to pretend to be engaged to me because I thought you would be a huge embarrassment as a fiancée.'

Shock gripped Poppy in a debilitating wave

only to be swiftly followed by a huge rush of hurt. 'In what way?'

'I was the posh bloke who made unjustified assumptions about you,' Gaetano admitted, his deep voice raw-edged with regret. 'I assumed you'd still be using a lot of bad language. I expected you to be totally lost and unable to cope in my world. In fact I believed that your eccentric fashion sense and everything about you would horrify Rodolfo and put him off the idea of me getting married, so that when the engagement broke down he would be relieved rather than disappointed...'

Gaetano had finished speaking but his every word still struck through the fog of Poppy's shell-shocked state like lightning on a dark stormy night. She felt physically sick.

Gaetano had watched the blood drain from below her skin and fierce tension now stamped his lean dark features. 'So that's the kind of guy I really am, the kind of guy you get to stay married to and the father of your future child. I know it's not pretty but you have earned the right to know the truth about me. Most of the time I'm an absolute bastard,' he stated bleakly. 'I tried to use you in the most callous way possible and it didn't once occur to me to wonder how that experience would ultimately affect you...or Rodolfo.'

Poppy wrapped her arms round her slim body as if she were trying to hold the dam of pain inside her back from breaking its banks. She couldn't bear to look at him any longer. He had seen from the outset how unworthy she was to be even his fiancée and he had planned to use her worst traits and the handicap of her poor background as an excuse to dump her again without antagonising his grandfather. In short he had handpicked her as the fake fiancée most likely to mortify him.

Poppy cringed inside herself. His prior assumptions appalled her, for she had not appreciated how prejudiced he had still been about her. Shattered by his admission, she felt humiliated beyond bearing. He had seen her flaws right at the

beginning and had pinned his hopes on her sham-
ing him. How could he then adapt to the idea of
staying married to her for years and years? Raising a child with her? Taking her out in public?

'The moment I picked you to fail was the moment that I sank to my all-time personal low,'
Gaetano confessed in a roughened undertone. 'I
got it horribly wrong. You *showed* me how wrong
my expectations were. You proved yourself to be
so much more than I was prepared for you to be
and I became ashamed of my original plan.'

'But you didn't need to tell me this once we
went as far as getting married,' she whispered
brokenly, backing in the direction of the door,
desperate to lick her wounds in private.

'You've always been honest with me. I'm trying to give you the same respect.'

'Only a couple of months ago you had *no* respect for me!' Poppy condemned with embittered
accuracy.

'That changed fast,' Gaetano fielded, moving
a step closer, wanting to hold her so badly and

resisting the urge with a frustration that coiled his big hands into fists. 'I *learned* to respect you. I learned a lot of other stuff from you as well.'

Feeling as though he were twisting a knife in her heart, Poppy voiced a loud sound of disagreement and snapped, 'You didn't learn anything… you never do. You're dumb as a rock about everything that really matters from giving Muffin a second chance at life to raising our child!' she accused. 'How could I ever trust you again?'

Poppy stalked out of the door and he fought his need to follow her. He didn't want her racing down the stairs and falling in an effort to evade him. 'Muffin trusts me,' he murmured flatly to the empty room. *Muffin?* Muffin who couldn't even tell him and Rodolfo apart? Admittedly, Muffin wasn't the sharpest tool in the box.

Gaetano groaned out loud. Maybe he should have kept on pretending to be a better man than he was but Poppy would only have found him out in the end. Poppy had a way of cutting through the nonsense to find the heart of an issue and see what really mattered. Just as Gaetano had finally seen what really mattered. Unfortunately that single instant of inner vision and comprehension had arrived with him pretty late in the day. He wasn't dumb as a rock about emotional stuff. He simply wasn't very practised at it. It wasn't something he'd ever bothered with until Poppy came along.

Poppy pelted out into the cool night. She needed air and space and silence to pull herself back together. The garden was softly lit, low-sited lights shining on exotic leaves and casting shadows in mysterious corners. Her face was wet with tears and she wiped her cheeks with angry hands. Damn him, damn him, damn him! What he had confessed had wounded her deeply. She loved Gaetano and he had always been her dream male. Handsome, brilliant, rich and glitzy, he had met every requirement for an adolescent fantasy. Now for the first time she was seeing herself through his eyes and it was so humiliating she wanted to sink into the earth and stay hidden there for ever.

He had only remembered the highly unsuitable bold girl with the potty mouth, and eccentric clothes, who could be depended on to embarrass him. And being Gaetano, who was never ever straightforward when he could be devious, manipulative and complicated instead, he had hoped to utilise her very obvious faults to frighten Rodolfo out of demanding that his grandson marry. And ironically, Rodolfo himself had set Poppy up for that fall by advising Gaetano to marry 'an ordinary girl'. And just how many ordinary girls did a jet-setter like Gaetano know?

None. Until Poppy had stumbled in that night at Woodfield Hall, to demand his attention and his non-existent compassion.

An embarrassment to him? No conventional dress sense, a dysfunctional family, no idea how to behave in rich, exclusive circles. Well, nothing had changed and she would never reach the high bar of social acceptability. Poppy shuddered, sick to her stomach with a galling sense of defeat and failure. She had never cared about such things but evidently Gaetano did. Even worse, Gaetano was currently offering to stay married to his unsuitable bride because she was pregnant.

She sat down on one of the cold stone seats sited round the table and her face burned hot in spite of the cool evening air when she remembered what had happened on that table only the day before. Gaetano was like an addiction, toxic, dangerous. He had gone from infuriating her to charming her to making her fall very deeply in love with him. And yet she had still never guessed how he really saw her. The gardener's daughter with the unfortunate family. It hurt— oh, my goodness, it *hurt*. But he had been right to tell her because she had needed to know the truth and accept it before she could stop weaving silly dreams about their future. So, how did she stay married to a male who had handpicked her to be an embarrassment?

The answer came swiftly. In such circumstances she could *not* stay married to Gaetano.

Regardless of her pregnancy, she needed to leave him and go ahead with a divorce.

'Poppy…'

Poppy stiffened. He must have walked across the grass because she would have heard his approach had he used the gravel paths. She breathed in deep, stiffening her facial muscles before she lifted her head.

'Should I have kept it a secret?' he asked her in a raw undertone.

He knew she was upset. His dark eyes were lingering on her, probably picking up on the dampness round her eyes even though she had quickly stopped crying. He noticed too much, *knew* too much about women. 'No,' she said heavily. 'It was better to tell me. I don't like you for it and it'll be hard to live with what I now know but you can't build a relationship on lies and pretences.'

Gaetano stilled in the shadow of the trees, his white shirt gleaming, his spectacular bone structure accentuated by the dim light. 'Don't leave me,' he framed unevenly. 'Even the idea of being without you scares me. I wouldn't like my life without you in it.'

Poppy couldn't imagine Gaetano being scared and she imagined his life would be a lot more normal and straightforward without her in it. Their child deserved better than to grow up with unhappily married and ill-matched parents. A divorce would be preferable to that. She would give Gaetano as much access as he wanted to their child but she didn't have to live with him or hang round his neck like an albatross to be a good parent. They could both commit to their child while living separately.

'I can't stay married to you,' she told him quietly. 'What would be the point?'

'I'm not good with emotions. I'm good at being angry, at being passionate, at being ambitious but I'm no good at the softer stuff. I lost that ability when I was a kid,' Gaetano admitted grittily. 'I loved my parents but they were incapable of loving me back and I saw that. I also saw that in comparison to them I felt *too* much. I learned to hide what I feel and eventually it became such a habit I didn't have to police myself any more. Emotion hurts. Rejection hurts, so I made sure I was safe by not feeling anything.'

Involuntarily, Poppy was touched that he was talking about his parents in an effort to bridge the chasm that had opened up between them. He never ever talked about his childhood but she would never forget his determined non-reaction when his dog had died, his stark refusal to betray any emotion. 'That makes sense,' she conceded.

'The only woman I ever loved after my mother left was my grandmother.'

'I thought at some stage you and *Serena*...'

'No. I walked away from her because I felt nothing and I knew there should be more.'

Poppy bowed her head, wondering why he was trying to stop her from walking away from him.

'I'm not quite as dumb as a rock,' Gaetano asserted heavily. 'But I was all screwed up about you long before we even got to the wedding.

Unfortunately marrying you only made me ten times more screwed up.'

'Screwed up?' Poppy queried, shifting uncomfortably on her hard stone seat.

'I got really involved with the wedding.'

'Yes, that was a surprise.'

'I wanted it to be special for you. I became very possessive of you. I assumed it was because we hadn't had sex.'

'Obviously,' Poppy chimed in because he seemed to expect it.

'In fact I was really only thinking in terms of sex.'

Poppy sent him a rather sad smile. 'I know that…it's basically your only means of communication in a relationship.'

'You're the only woman I've ever had a relationship with.'

Poppy stared at him, green eyes luminous in the light. 'How can you say that with your reputation?'

'All those weeks after your illness when I didn't

touch you but we were together all the time…that was like my version of dating,' Gaetano told her darkly. 'The affairs I had with women before you went no further than dinner followed by sex or the theatre followed by sex or—'

'OK…I've got the picture,' she cut in hurriedly, her gaze clinging to the dark beauty of his bronzed features with growing fascination. 'So…your version of dating?'

'I wanted to get to know you—'

'No, you were on a massive guilt trip because I fell ill. That's why you didn't sleep with me again and why you spent so much time entertaining me.'

'I'm not a masochist. I spent so much time with you because I was enjoying myself,' Gaetano contradicted. 'And I didn't touch you again because I didn't want to be selfish. I thought you would be happier if I made no further demands.'

Poppy sent him a withering appraisal. 'You got it wrong.'

'Poppy…let's face it,' Gaetano muttered heavily. 'I got *everything* wrong with you.'

Her tender heart reacted with a first shard of genuine sympathy. 'No, the sex was ten out of ten and your version of dating was amazingly engaging. You made me happy, Gaetano. You definitely win points for that.'

'I bought you something today and it wasn't until I bought it and realised what it symbolised that I finally understood myself,' he framed harshly, pulling a tiny box from his pocket.

Poppy studied the fancy logo of a world-famous jeweller with surprised eyes and opened the box. It was a ring, a continuous circlet of diamonds that flashed like fire in the artificial light. She blinked down at it in confusion.

'It's an eternity ring,' Gaetano pointed out very quietly.

A laugh that wasn't a laugh at all was wrenched from Poppy. 'Kind of an odd choice when before you came home and I made my announcement you were set on eventually getting a divorce,' she pointed out.

'But it expresses how I feel.' Gaetano cleared his throat in obvious discomfiture. 'When you talk about leaving me, it tears me apart. Because somewhere along the line, somehow, I fell in love with you, Poppy. I know it's love because I've never felt like this before and the idea of losing you terrifies me.'

'Love...' Poppy whispered shakily.

'Never thought it could happen to me,' Gaetano confided in a rush. 'I didn't want it to happen either. I didn't want to get attached to anyone and then you came along and you were so perfect I couldn't resist you.'

'P-perfect?' she stammered in a daze.

Gaetano dropped down on his knees in the dew-wet grass and reached for her hand. He tugged off the engagement ring and threaded on the eternity ring so that it rested beside her wedding ring. 'You're perfect for me. You get who I am, even with my faults. The money doesn't get in the way for you, doesn't impress you. You keep me grounded. You make me unbelievably happy. You make me question my actions and really think about what I'm doing,' he bit out. 'With you, I'm something more, something better, and I need that. I need you in my life.'

Her lashes fluttered. She could hear him but she couldn't quite believe him, there on his knees at her feet, his hand trembling slightly in hers because he was scared, he was scared she wouldn't listen, wouldn't accept that he really loved her. And that fear touched her down deep inside, wrapping round her crazy fears about Serena and the terrible insecurities that had sent her running out of the house and sealing them for ever. Suddenly none of that existed because Gaetano *loved* her, Gaetano *needed* her…

'I love you so much. I couldn't stand to lose you and my first thought when you told me you were pregnant was, "She'll stay now," and it was a massive relief to think that even though you didn't love me you would stay so that we could bring up our child together.'

'I do love you,' Poppy murmured intently, leaning forward to kiss him.

'You're not just saying it because I said it first?' Gaetano checked.

'I really, *really* love you.'

'Even though I don't have a single loveable trait?' he quoted back at her quick as a flash.

'You grew on me like mould,' Poppy told him deadpan.

Gaetano burst out laughing and sprang upright, pulling her up into the circle of his arms. 'Like mould?' he queried.

Poppy looked up into his beautiful eyes and her heart did a happy dance inside her. 'I like cheese,' she proclaimed defensively.

'Do you like your ring?'

'Very much,' she told him instantly, smiling up at him with a true sense of joyful possessiveness. 'But I like what it symbolises most of all. You didn't want to let me go, you wanted to keep me.'

'And I intend to keep you for ever and ever. Anything less than eternity wouldn't be enough, *amata mia.*'

'The baby was a shock, wasn't it?' She sighed, walking back towards the house with him hand in hand.

'A wonderful one. Our little miracle,' Gaetano said with sudden rueful humour. 'It took one hell of a baby to get in under my radar, so I'll be expecting a very determined personality in the family.'

Gaetano halted at that point to claim a kiss. And Poppy threw herself into that kiss with abandon. He pressed her back against a tree trunk, his body hard and urgent against hers and a rippling shudder of excitement shimmied through her slender length.

'Let's go to bed,' she suggested, looking up at him with bold appreciative eyes.

'We haven't had dinner yet and a mother-to-be needs sustenance,' Gaetano told her lazily, trailing her indoors and out to the terrace where the table awaited them.

But neither of them ate very much. Between the intense looks exchanged and the suggestive conversation, it wasn't very long before they headed upstairs at a very adult stately pace, which broke down into giggles and a clumsy embrace as Poppy rugby-tackled Gaetano down onto the floor of their bedroom. By the time they made it to the bed and he had moved the suitcase she had left there they were kissing passionately and holding each other so tightly that it was a challenge to remove clothes. But they managed through kisses and caresses and mutual promises to make love with all the fire and excitement that powered them both and afterwards they lay with their arms wrapped round each other, secure in their love and talking about their future.

Poppy glanced out of the front window and saw her children with Rodolfo. Sarah was holding his hand and chattering, her little face animated below her halo of red curls. Benito was pedalling his trike doggedly in front of them, ignoring the fact that the deep gravel on the path made cycling a challenge for a little boy.

Sarah was four years old and took after her mother in looks and her father in nature. She already knew all her numbers, was very much a thinking child and tended to look after her little brother in a bossy way. Benito was two, dark of hair and eye and as lively as a jumping bean. He was on the go from dawn to dusk and generally fell asleep during his bedtime story in his father's arms.

Sometimes, or at least until she looked at her expanding family, Poppy found it hard to credit that she had been married for five years. Gaetano might have been a late convert to family life but he had taken to it like the proverbial duck to water. He adored his children and rushed home to be with them and it was thanks to his persuasion that Poppy was carrying their third child. Third and last, she had told him firmly even though she liked the way their family had developed. In retrospect she was glad they hadn't waited and that Sarah had taken them by surprise and not having too big a gap between the children meant that they could grow up with each other.

But, at the same time, Poppy was also looking forward to having more time to devote to her own interests. She had taken several landscape designer courses over the years and was planning to set up a small landscaping firm. She had redesigned the gardens at La Fattoria to make them more child-friendly and had already taken several private commissions from friends, one of which had won an award. The gardens at the London town house and at Woodfield Hall both bore her stamp and when she wanted to relax she was usually to be found in a greenhouse tending the rare orchids she collected.

Gaetano was CEO of the Leonetti Bank and when he travelled, Poppy and the children often went with him. He put his family first and at the heart of his life, ensuring that they took lengthy breaks abroad to wind down from their busy lives. Poppy's mother, Jasmine, had made a good recovery and was now training as an addiction counsellor to help others as she had been helped. She lived in Manchester with her sister but she was a frequent visitor in London, as was Poppy's brother. Damien, backed by Gaetano, had recently started up a specialist motorcycle repair shop.

In fact there wasn't a cloud in Poppy's sky because she was happy. Sadly, Muffin had passed away of old age the year before and he had been replaced by a rescued golden Labrador who enjoyed rough and tumble games with the children.

'Guess who...' A pair of hands covered her eyes while a lean, hard body connected with hers.

Poppy grinned. The familiar scent of Gaetano's cologne assailed her while his hands travelled places nobody else would have dared. 'You're the only sex pest I know,' she teased, suppressing a moan as the hand that had splayed across her slightly swollen belly snaked lower and circled, sending sweet sensation snaking through her responsive body.

Gaetano spun his wife round and she reached up to wind her arms round his neck. 'Sorry, I slept in this morning and missed seeing you.'

'You were up with Benito last night when he had a nightmare, *amata mia*,' he reminded her. 'That's why I didn't wake you.'

Poppy teased the corner of his wide sensual mouth with her own, heat warming her core. She wanted to drag him to the bed and ravish him. Her hunger for him never went entirely away. He shrugged off his jacket and stared down at her with smouldering dark golden eyes. 'Share the shower with me...'

'Promise not to get my hair wet,' she bargained.

'You know I can't.' An unholy grin slashed Gaetano's lips. 'Sometimes you get carried away. Is that my fault?'

'Absolutely your fault,' his wife told him as she peeled off her dress.

Gaetano treated her to a fiercely appreciative

appraisal. 'Did I ever tell you how amazingly sexy you look when you're pregnant?'

'You may have mentioned it once or twice—'

'Sometimes I can hardly believe you're mine. I love you so much, *amata mia*,' Gaetano swore passionately, gathering her up into his arms with care and kissing her breathless.

'I love you too,' she said between kisses, happiness bubbling through her at the sure knowledge that she was going to get her hair very wet indeed.

* * * * *

MILLS & BOON®
Large Print – June 2016

Leonetti's Housekeeper Bride
Lynne Graham

The Surprise De Angelis Baby
Cathy Williams

Castelli's Virgin Widow
Caitlin Crews

The Consequence He Must Claim
Dani Collins

Helios Crowns His Mistress
Michelle Smart

Illicit Night with the Greek
Susanna Carr

The Sheikh's Pregnant Prisoner
Tara Pammi

Saved by the CEO
Barbara Wallace

Pregnant with a Royal Baby!
Susan Meier

A Deal to Mend Their Marriage
Michelle Douglas

Swept into the Rich Man's World
Katrina Cudmore

0516 Rom LP

MILLS & BOON®
Large Print – July 2016

The Italian's Ruthless Seduction
Miranda Lee

Awakened by Her Desert Captor
Abby Green

A Forbidden Temptation
Anne Mather

A Vow to Secure His Legacy
Annie West

Carrying the King's Pride
Jennifer Hayward

Bound to the Tuscan Billionaire
Susan Stephens

Required to Wear the Tycoon's Ring
Maggie Cox

The Greek's Ready-Made Wife
Jennifer Faye

Crown Prince's Chosen Bride
Kandy Shepherd

Billionaire, Boss...Bridegroom?
Kate Hardy

Married for Their Miracle Baby
Soraya Lane